The Football Spy

The Charlie Fry Series Part Four

Martin Smith

For Steven and Mark, who never let me
win during those long-gone summers.

CONTENTS

Note from the author

Acknowledgments

Other books by Martin Smith

1. GOALS GALORE

"Run!"

Charlie Fry did not need to be told twice.

Legs pumping at full speed, the Magpies striker eased past the last defender and chased the through ball.

The goalkeeper was coming out to try to claim the ball but he had made the wrong decision.

He was too far away and would never reach it.

Charlie could feel his heart racing as he flew towards Wootton Pools goal.

Excitement was building inside him again – the Football Boy Wonder loved the magical feeling of scoring goals.

And he was scoring a lot.

"You can make it, Charlie!"

Emma Tysoe's voice was distant now.

Her pass had been perfectly placed into the large space between the Wootton defenders and the goalkeeper.

Charlie did not need encouragement.

He knew what to do. He did not hesitate.

Scoring goals had become a habit.

His black boot brought the ball neatly under

control and deliberately pushed it towards his favoured right foot.

Happy the ball was exactly where he wanted it; Charlie took a quick look up towards the Wootton goal.

The goalkeeper stopped and began to desperately back track as he realised his mistake.

But it was too late.

He had made Charlie's life a lot easier.

"Watch out for the chip!"

One of the defenders cried out the warning to the Wootton goalkeeper but the error had already been made.

Charlie did not even have to chip him.

With the blink of his eye, he locked the magic target floating in his eyesight into the bottom right corner of the goal.

It flashed green to confirm the lock and Charlie casually side-footed the ball towards the corner of the net.

He struck the ball firmly with a hint of curl.

The keeper, now back inside his penalty area, dived at full stretch to his left.

The shot though was perfectly placed.

It went past the boy's despairing dive, only a couple of centimetres away from his outstretched finger-tips.

The ball flew along the floor until finally nestling in the corner of the Wootton net.

GOAL!

Charlie Fry was moving towards the Magpies supporters even before the ball reached the net.

The 11-year-old jumped high into the air in celebration, arms raised above his head as the crowd cheered.

His short blonde hair was soaked with sweat.

It was a late March afternoon but the day felt like summer.

It was a perfect day for football.

Nothing can beat the feeling that football gives you, he thought as the crowd celebrated in front of him.

He had never seen such numbers on the side-lines before.

They knew something special was happening this season.

Charlie closed his eyes and enjoyed the moment.

He was back.

After a two-week spell in hospital just before Christmas, he felt great.

It had taken him a few weeks to get his fitness back but he was now flying.

Luckily, weeks of bad winter weather had forced matches to be postponed so he had only missed one game for Magpies.

The illness had taught him an important lesson.

He could not ignore the fact he had cystic fibrosis.

He needed to be smart. That meant doing physio every day to clear his poorly lungs and taking his medication at the right time.

Since he had come out of hospital, he had followed the doctor's orders to the letter – and he'd never felt better.

Charlie was determined not miss any more football if he could avoid it.

"I knew you'd reach it!"

Emma – the team's flying winger – crashed into her teammate, throwing both arms around him in celebration.

Charlie turned around with a huge smile and the friends hugged as the rest of the team raced to congratulate the Football Boy Wonder on another goal.

He had scored four goals in today's match alone.

And he wanted more.

Charlie had 21 goals this season and he wanted to be top goal-scorer in the division.

He could not stop scoring at the moment.

Only bully-boy Adam Knight and Charlie's buddy Brian Bishop had scored more than him.

They were equal top of the goal-scoring charts with 25 each.

Charlie could easily close that gap – and most likely beat them.

Magpies were the in-form team at the moment.

They won every time they played.

And both Adam's Thrapborough Colts and Bishop's Hall Park Rovers had been stuttering in recent weeks.

Magpies could still catch them and win the league.

After all, they still had to play Colts and Rovers in the final few games of the season.

And every time they ran on to the pitch, it felt … right.

Charlie could not explain why, but they had clicked as a team.

They felt they could beat anyone nowadays.

Magpies had come a long way in only a few months.

"Er, Mr Boy Wonder? Can someone else have a go please?"

Peter Bell pushed the others out of the way and

grabbed his best mate in a big bear hug.

The embrace seemed to last forever – Charlie could not stop laughing as Peter refused to let go of his grip.

Finally he released Charlie.

Smoothing his crumpled shirt, Charlie replied: "Maybe if you stopped doing your hair and played the game, then you'd be on the score-sheet, Belly."

Peter punched the Boy Wonder on the arm playfully as they began walking back to the centre circle for the restart.

"Shut up! Who keeps making these chances for you?"

Charlie opened his mouth but was beaten to the reply.

"That would be me!" Emma flung her arms around both of the boys' shoulders as they laughed together.

Life was good.

The score was 7-0 to Magpies, a small piece of revenge for the 5-0 drubbing that Wootton had dished out to them earlier in the season.

That had been before Charlie had joined though.

It had been before Peter had returned.

It had happened before wing wizard Emma and goalkeeping legend Mudder had signed up.

And it was weeks before the magic football book had begun to correctly predict victories for the Hall Park team every week.

Times had changed.

Back in the autumn, Magpies' Under-13s were the league's whipping boys but they were now unstoppable.

It was not even half-time.

The Wootton players looked like they'd had enough already.

Charlie grinned at his parents as they applauded the jubilant Magpies players.

It was quickly becoming a season none of them would ever forget.

And the Football Boy Wonder was the star of the show – and everyone knew it.

2. FAME

Bang! Bang! Bang!

A large fist thumped heavily against the front door.

Charlie groaned and pulled the duvet over his head.

He did not want to get up.

He was tired after yesterday's match – and the celebrations afterwards.

His warm bed was so comfortable but the caller was not going away.

Charlie had ignored the doorbell three times already.

Now they were banging on the front door.

It must be important, he thought, as he rubbed sleep out of his eyes.

Charlie sat up in bed and looked at the football clock that sat on the desk across from his bed.

8.14am.

"Urrghhh!" Charlie grunted and flopped back down on his bed.

It was far too early.

Why couldn't his mum answer the door?

Then he remembered: she would have taken his little brother Harry to junior hockey ages ago.

His dad would be in the back garden as always so he would not be able to hear the knocking.

That left Charlie.

Bang!

"Alright!" Charlie shouted angrily, fully aware the caller would not be able to hear him.

He pushed his hands through his spiky blonde hair to try to wake up a touch more.

With an effort, Charlie stood up and grabbed the well-worn Blues dressing gown from the peg on his door.

He then pulled on his football shaped slippers and trudged down the stairs, grumbling to himself as he went.

He opened the door to find two men, who had their backs to him and were slowly walking away from the house.

Charlie sighed.

If he had waited just a little longer, they would have given up and left him in peace. He could have got away with it.

But he was up now.

"Er ... hello?"

Charlie watched as the men span around.

The man closest to him responded with a huge grin stretching across his chubby face.

"Ah, Charlie! Great to see you – we thought no-one was home."

The man had dark stubble over his chin, neatly trimmed black hair and looked a little tubby around the waist.

He had big shoulders – Charlie guessed he was probably a keen swimmer in his younger years – and was wearing a white shirt and black trousers.

In his hand was an ancient mobile phone, which he held out in front of him as he spoke.

"My name is Andrew Hallmaker. I am a senior reporter with the Crickledon Telegraph."

Charlie crinkled his nose. The press?

Hallmaker continued: "And this is my colleague, the award-winning photographer Jimmy Baffour. Everyone calls him 'Flex' though."

Flex waved a greeting but did not say anything more.

Charlie could see the expensive camera in his hands and a huge knot in his tie that took up most of his chest.

Charlie scrunched his face up with confusion. But he did not have the time to ask any questions. Hallmaker had not finished.

"We just wanted a few words with yourself ... and your parents, of course," Hallmaker said as he peered over Charlie's shoulder into the house.

Charlie saw an opportunity.

"No, they're not here. They're at the hockey with my little brother," he lied.

Hallmaker looked disappointed.

He turned and nodded to Flex, who pulled a phone out of his pocket as he walked towards a black car parked on the road nearby.

As Flex carefully placed his camera bag into the car's boot, Hallmaker turned back to face Charlie once more.

"Oh, that's rubbish. We can't interview you, Charlie, without your parents' permission. You are too young, you see."

"Take a card, Charlie, and give it your mum and dad. We would love to interview you for the Telegraph."

The journalist fished out a small mangled card with his name and phone number on it.

He held the business card against his chest for a moment to try to flatten it out a little before handing it to Charlie.

"Er, Mr Hallmaker, what did you want to talk about?"

Charlie's head was spinning. It was too early for this.

Hallmaker laughed.

"We want to do a story about you, Charlie. Your name is the one on everyone's lips according to our news editor Stevie Chilton.

"Even Coops says you're the best footballer that Crickledon and Hall Park has ever produced. The big clubs are watching you, Mr Boy Wonder."

Charlie's heart skipped a beat.

"What? Have the Blues watched me?"

Hallmaker placed a hand on Charlie's shoulder and spoke in a low voice.

"No, they haven't. But almost every other big club in the Premier League are watching, Charlie Fry. They're expecting big things from you. We all are."

3. THE SPY

Chell Di Santos sat in his office trying to ignore the pesky fly buzzing around his head.

He had spent the last 10 minutes reading the full-page article in the Crickledon Telegraph about Charlie Fry.

The Hall Park Rovers boss had read the story twice and could feel his rage rising with every word.

His bony fingers wrapped around the newspaper and crinkled it into a ball, which he flung across the room.

The mangled paper flew into one of the trophies positioned in the corner of the room and it fell to the floor.

Deep in thought, Di Santos pushed a hand through his long black hair that was immaculately slicked back.

Charlie Fry and Hall Park Magpies were becoming a bigger problem every week.

Even stealing their excellent goalkeeper Sam Walker had not stopped them like he had planned.

From somewhere and against all the odds, Magpies had found a replacement.

To make matters worse, Darren Bunnell was even better than Walker.

With Bunnell performing miracles in goal and that show-off Fry up front, they were rapidly catching Di Santos's Rovers team.

Di Santos's lips curled into a sneer as the Boy Wonder flashed into his thoughts.

He never seemed to escape The Boy Who Could Not Miss.

The Rovers manager's fingers noisily tapped the keyboard on his desk, typing the website address for the Crickledon Under-13s league tables.

In a flash, the information was sitting in front of him.

He already knew what was on the screen in front of him.

Rovers were clear at the top. A point behind were Thrapborough Colts with Magpies in third – five points behind Rovers.

It was close, too close.

Chell Di Santos's hands curled into fists. He made a half-hearted attempt to swat the fly but he missed again.

Barney Payne's team were charging up the table.

How could this happen?

Only a few months ago they had looked finished.

Bottom of the table, losing every game and with not enough players, Di Santos was certain they would fold before Christmas.

But it hadn't worked out like that.

To make things worse, Rovers had stopped winning.

As Magpies had begun sweeping aside every team they faced, his side had forgotten how to score goals.

They had thrown away points for weeks. And then last weekend, Rovers had lost their first game of the season.

Luckily their rivals Thrapborough had also stuttered, meaning Rovers had remained top of the league.

But something had to be done.

He had to win the league.

His reputation depended on it. His career demanded it. If he was to reach the Premier League, he needed to be a winner.

Di Santos had already decided to recall Joe Foster as Rovers' number one goalkeeper.

The boy was hugely talented, Di Santos knew.

Sam Walker was a decent keeper – but he needed his best players if he was going to win the league.

Di Santos had happily dropped him earlier in the season for one reason: he was Charlie Fry's best friend.

But it had been a big mistake.

He did not understand how that irritating oik Charlie Fry had managed to score so many goals. He could not even run!

What was his secret?

The fly was back. It landed on the computer screen as Di Santos gazed at the league table, deep in thought.

A ghostly white finger snaked out and crushed the insect with a deadly flick.

Di Santos pulled out a tissue from the pocket in his black suit jacket and wiped away the squashed fly from his fingers.

And then he realised what he needed to do.

Di Santos pulled out his phone, searching for a

number in the contacts list before hitting the call button.

His lips peeled back into a horrid smile as he spoke.

"It is me. I have an offer for you.

"Help me and I will give you what you want."

As the person at the other end of the line replied, Di Santos's attention returned to the remains of the dead fly on his computer screen.

He grinned again: "Excellent. You will be Hall Park Rovers next signing if you complete your part of the deal.

"All I need is one thing.

"It is very simple.

"Very easy.

"I want to know Charlie Fry's secret."

Chell Di Santos grinned, revealing horrible yellow teeth.

Charlie Fry simply needed to be squashed once and for all – just like an annoying bug.

4. DISCOVERED

"What did you say to him?"

Peter could not keep the amazement out of his voice.

"Nothing!" Charlie shot back at Peter despite unable to take his eyes off the phone screen sitting in Joe Foster's hand.

The three friends were huddled together on a wooden bench at The Rec.

It was early evening and they had arranged to play a game of headers and volleys.

Toby, Annie, Emma, Wrecka, Bishop and Mudder hadn't turned up yet so the boys were waiting for them to arrive.

Even though it was early spring, the park was bathed in bright sunshine.

For almost a week, the days had been boiling hot – Peter was even wearing shorts.

Charlie, of course, was not so quick to ditch his jog bottoms.

He had been feeling great over the past couple of

months after his two-week spell in hospital.

But Charlie knew he had to be careful. If he tried to ignore his cystic fibrosis again, then he would fall ill once more.

He needed to keep warm and healthy – Magpies relied on him to be sensible.

Peter stood up on the concrete path and turned to face his pals.

"So the Crickledon Telegraph turned up at your door, had a chat and then printed this story – without any words from you?"

Charlie was still reading the article over Joe's shoulder.

Premier League eye Crickledon Football Boy Wonder

Exclusive by Andrew Hallmaker

Crickledon's Football Boy Wonder Charlie Fry is the number one target for a string of Premier League clubs.

The Crickledon Telegraph can exclusively reveal 15 scouts from England's top division saw the budding soccer superstar score six goals last weekend.

United, City and Rovers scouts watched Fry claim a double hat-trick as rampant Hall Park Magpies Under-13s team continues its fine form.

The 11-year-old – dubbed the Football Boy Wonder by Hall Park fans – looks certain to seal a move to the Premier League in the summer.

The Telegraph understands Fry would prefer a move to the Blues ahead of their rivals. However their scouts have yet to check on Crickledon's new superstar.

Hall Park old boy and local football legend Johnny Cooper has been a regular on the sidelines at Magpies' matches this season.

Cooper, whose daughter Annie also plays for Magpies, said: "He is a star already. He will play in the Premier League and will captain England. He's that good.

"We all know he can't run too far but Charlie never complains. And when he gets the ball, he is lethal – the best I have ever seen."

Hall Park are fully aware the hugely talented striker is unlikely to stay with them for much longer.

A club spokesman told the Telegraph that Fry had "great talent and potential" but was part of a team that "oozed quality and determination".

Charlie could barely believe it. Were they really talking about him?

United? City? Rovers?

Where were his beloved Blues?

His mind was whirring.

"Planet Earth to Charlie Fry! Wake up, Mr Big Shot!"

Peter booted the ball into Charlie's stomach and stopped the daydream in its tracks. Charlie groaned and rubbed his tummy.

"What was that for?"

"Because you had disappeared into a strange little dream world, probably imagining you were playing in the Premier League!" Joe interrupted as he put the phone back into his backpack and pulled out his gloves.

Peter laughed and walked to pick up the ball that had bounced a couple of metres away from them.

"You do remember this Hallmaker chap is the guy who wrote loads of rubbish about you before Christmas?

"He's a chump! Why didn't you tell us he had knocked on your door? And what did you say to him?"

Charlie frowned with concentration.

What had he said to the reporter?

He could barely remember – it was almost a week ago now and he had been half asleep at the time.

Charlie shook his head.

"No, he's okay. I didn't say anything. Apart from…."

"What?" Joe and Peter spoke together.

Charlie blushed. "… asking if the Blues had been to one of our games. And he said they hadn't."

Peter blew out his cheeks.

"Well that's not too bad. If these guys realised what a complete dipstick you are, it could have been a lot worse."

Peter never changed – he took the mickey out of everyone, whether you were his best friend or a complete stranger.

Joe stood still, gazing across the freshly cut grass as he ignored the banter.

Finally he turned to face his two friends.

"Do you think they know?"

Charlie returned his stare. "About me?"

Joe nodded.

Peter snorted.

"How could they?"

Joe twitched his lips and turned back to the grassy field.

"It seems like they are paying a lot of attention to Charlie all of a sudden.

"I know he is scoring lots of goals but the whole Magpies team is scoring yet everyone is obsessed with him.

"It is odd."

Charlie moved closer to his oldest friend.

Peter followed so they were standing in a tight group.

Charlie shook his head as he spoke.

"Only you and Belly know.

"That's the way it is going to stay.

"It is our secret and no-one else will ever know."

A familiar voice spoke up behind them, making all three boys jump.

"What secret?"

5. FOUND OUT

Annie Cooper stood a couple of metres away from the boys, who were all uneasily looking at the floor.

Wearing her Hall Park top and black leggings, Annie was staring straight at Charlie as she waited for an answer.

Charlie and Annie – the daughter of Johnny Cooper, Hall Park's best ever player – were friends.

She had saved his football career a few months ago.

It had been Annie who had convinced her dad to give Charlie a chance at Magpies after evil Chell Di Santos had shown him the door at Hall Park Rovers.

Charlie owed her – and he hated to lie to his friend.

"What secret?"

Annie repeated the question. She sounded angry too.

Peter spoke first.

"You know, it is just boring boy talk. It is nothing more. It wouldn't interest a big girl like you."

Annie snapped back immediately: "Don't give me that rubbish. I asked Charlie, not you."

Peter looked stunned and did not respond.

Annie turned her glare back on Charlie, flicking her long, brown ponytail as she cocked her head to one side: "You three are always whispering together. Something is going on and I want to know what it is."

Charlie swallowed.

She was right.

Annie deserved to know.

"No, Charlie." Joe shook his head in warning.

"I trust her, Joe. She needs to know. She is my friend too."

Annie moved closer. She now looked less angry and more concerned.

"Charlie?"

She put a hand on his arm. "Tell me."

Charlie took a deep breath.

"I was hit by a lightning bolt the summer before we met. Do you remember the early autumn storm last year?"

Annie nodded but did not speak to allow Charlie to continue.

"When the lightning hit me, I was on my phone.

"I am not sure how it happened but somehow the target from my football game app ... ended up inside my head."

Charlie paused.

He thought she would interrupt at this point and call his story a load of nonsense.

Instead, she waited for him to finish.

Charlie continued: "And this target ... well, it means I can't miss.

"Wherever I put it, the ball will go – as long as I

kick it hard enough.

"It is why I score so many goals."

He stopped and realised he felt tired. Something had changed though. It felt like a weight had been lifted from his shoulders.

Charlie should have told Annie sooner.

She took his hand gently.

"Charlie Fry. I don't believe in magic targets but I do believe in you. Magic target or not, you are someone special. And don't forget it."

Charlie beamed as they hugged.

"What is going on? I thought we were playing football, not spending the evening hugging each other?"

Emma Tysoe's voice boomed out from behind them, as she walked towards the group with a big smile.

"And look who I found lurking behind the trees!"

Toby Grace stepped out from behind the tree.

The small boy blushed as he waved to his friends but did not speak.

Toby made an unsuccessful attempt to push down the shock of short brown hair sticking up at the back of his head before he followed Emma as the others began moving on to the grass to start the game.

6. THE BOOK

"So Hall Park Magpies, we're back on home turf at last."

Barney Payne's team had played the last three matches away from Manor Park.

After three convincing wins, they were back at their home ground. The place looked completely different.

The dripping shower and rotting benches had gone.

Fresh wooden seats and newly painted walls welcomed the Magpies Under-13s team as they arrived for the lunchtime kick-off.

There had been changes on the pitch too.

The grass had been freshly cut and there was no sign of dog poo anywhere. Crowds were already starting to build around the pitch.

Manor Park had never really been a football ground. It was a popular park in Crickledon with a football pitch wedged into the spare space.

Magpies had changed that.

They were now the talk of the town.

Everyone wanted to see the team that could not stop scoring – and watch the boy that was being tipped to become England captain.

Barney looked round his team.

"We need to keep our focus. Hulcote United are a decent side.

"We may have leapfrogged them in the league but do not underestimate them.

"Their wingers are quick so keep a close eye on them."

Charlie, sitting on the bench next to Toby, winced.

He remembered playing Hulcote when he was a Hall Park Rovers player.

One of their nippy wingers, a lad called Ben, had run rings around him that day, and Charlie had been humiliatingly subbed after only six minutes.

His face reddened at the thought of the absolute nightmare caused by Chell Di Santos all those months ago.

Charlie promised himself silently that Hulcote would see the real Football Boy Wonder in action today.

"Er, Boss?"

Mike Parson stood up. Mike was Magpies' captain and everyone called him Wrecka.

Barney paused.

"Yes, Wrecka?"

Wrecka stood next to the coach and turned to face the rest of the team.

No-one said a word.

Every set of eyes in the changing room were fixed upon the captain.

Looking at Barney, Wrecka said: "Gaffer, let me

finish this team talk for you."

Barney smiled and nodded his permission.

In his loudest voice, the captain roared: "Who is going to win today?"

The response was instant: "Magpies!"

Wrecka shook his head.

"I can't hear you! Who is going to win again?"

The answer this time was deafening.

"MAGPIES!"

Wrecka broke into a big grin as the squad burst into laughter – before he turned his full attention back to Barney.

"I think we have enough focus, gaffer. I have one more question though: what does our magic football book predict today?"

The team went quiet once more and waited for Barney to reveal the book's latest prediction.

Since Annie's dad Coops had introduced the book to the team – it had never been wrong.

Sometimes it gave the correct score, other times just the result.

Either way, it was always right.

Barney nodded his head.

"Good question. The answer is I can't tell you."

There was a gasp around the room.

Annie blurted out the obvious question.

"Why not? Where's the book?"

Barney shrugged.

"It is here but your father has it and he has just taken an urgent call.

"If he doesn't come back before kick-off, I'll get him to come into our half-time team talk. Sound fair?"

The numerous nods and mutters of agreement

revealed the team was happy with the arrangement.

He spoke again: "Now, who is ready to win today?"

The roar in response told the manager all he needed to know.

Hall Park Magpies were ready.

7. RESPECT

Barney watched the game from the touchline. He enjoyed every second.

His pride was obvious.

He was near the end of his coaching career and thought he had seen everything in the game.

Then this team came along. He could not explain it. Magpies Under-13s were special.

Nowadays, they barely needed a manager. His tactics were not needed.

All they required was a calming word, the odd telling off and someone to pin the team sheet on the wall each week.

And they kept getting better.

The score line was 6-0 to Magpies and it was only 10 minutes into the second half. It had been a footballing master-class.

Charlie had scored four goals inside the first 15 minutes. Hulcote had been beaten before half-time.

Now it was a case of how many.

Barney leapt into the air as Peter unleashed a shot

from outside the box but saw it whistle just over the bar.

His eyes scanned the rest of the team. They were all smiling as they played this incredible football with friends.

Barney allowed himself a little smile too.

His players were good kids.

There was no showing off or taking the mickey out of players, even when Magpies were handing out thrashings every week.

"Could the boy cut it in the Premier League, Payne?"

A familiar voice spoke in a low whisper, causing Barney to jump and turn his attention away from the game.

Deano Webb was the main youth scout for United. It was the third time in a month he had watched Magpies play.

Barney had got to know the scout well over the years.

Deano was dressed like he was going to the beach – a shirt with only one button done up, baggy shorts and flip flops.

Barney had never seen him wear a coat even in the darkest days of January. His black hair was always messy and his stubble overgrown.

Yet he was the number one scout in the country.

He was known throughout the game for finding the best young players and taking them to the very top.

Deano Webb was a man who understood soccer.

Barney kept his eyes fixed on the pitch shrugged. "Perhaps, he is some player. Can't we talk later, Deano? There's a game going on."

Deano ignored Barney's request.

"Is he strong enough mentally?

"And can his health cope at the top level?"

Barney frowned and turned away from the game.

"I don't know. His health is an issue. He has cystic fibrosis – it is not something you just get over. We have to be careful with him."

Deano looked around to ensure no-one could hear the conversation.

Barney knew the scout was concerned about other clubs making a move for Charlie first.

"But…."

Barney held up a hand to interrupt him.

"Wait, I hadn't finished. Let's get this straight: he's the best young player I have ever seen.

"In fact, he is the best player I have ever seen in almost 50 years of coaching.

"They call him the Football Boy Wonder and they're right.

"He is sensational. He needs to be treated differently because of his health but he is mentally strong and will never – willingly – ask for special treatment.

"He is a risk, of course, but he is definitely good enough for United.

"In fact, I think he would be in the first team at 16, perhaps even earlier."

Barney finished his sentence and watched Webb's reaction.

The scout could not hide his surprise.

Barney knew why.

He rarely praised any one highly. But he never lied either and Charlie Fry deserved to be considered for the Premier League.

Webb puffed out his cheeks.

"Will you pass on my details to him please?"

The scout held out his card. Barney reached out to take the business card on offer.

Deano nodded his thanks and drifted back into the throng of spectators to watch the rest of the game.

Cheering from the crowd caused the Magpies manager to turn back to the game in a flash.

"Olé, Olé, Olé!"

Annie and Peter were flicking the ball to each other, keeping it off the ground as they ran down the wing.

The crowd was enjoying the tricks as Magpies enjoyed the win.

But Barney's face went bright red.

He hated showboating.

"Stop that … RIGHT NOW!"

He bellowed the order out across the pitch, causing several spectators standing nearby to jump with surprise.

Barney looked along the touchline at Magpies' two substitutes, who were half-heartedly stretching at the far end of the pitch.

Since they had begun to win games, kids wanted to play for Magpies again. It was the Football Boy Wonder Factor, as Coops had described it.

Barney shielded his eyes to get a better look at the two boys talking in the sunshine.

Jimmy Welford was a decent tall goalkeeper with long shoulder-length blonde hair and a strange taste in pink boots.

He looked more like a surfer than a footballer.

But today he would be playing on the pitch – whether he liked it or not.

Paul Flemmell had his back to Barney.

His dad had brought him to training because he wanted to get his boy away from the computer and playing outside.

Paul – or 'Flem' as the team called him – was a nice lad.

He was really keen but he took a lot of flak from the others – mainly because he had the strangest haircut ever.

He looked like someone had wonkily placed a big bowl around his head and then grabbed a pair of garden shears to do the rest.

"Ted, get Jimmy and Flem ready.

"I want those two idiots taken off. NOW!"

As Barney waved his arms to attract the referee's attention, a small white card fluttered to the ground already forgotten.

Deano Webb's business card was trampled into the Manor Park turf and no-one gave it a second glance.

8. ASHAMED

Barney stood in the middle of the packed changing room.

There was silence. The mood of the manager told them that it was not a time for celebration.

Peter and Annie sat together, looking glum-faced.

The Under-13s manager had not spoken to either of them since he had subbed them in the second half.

Barney was not happy.

He ran his hands through his white hair and straightened out his black tracksuit top as he made the team wait.

Finally he spoke.

"Well done, Magpies. To beat Hulcote by eight goals to nil is hugely impressive.

"And a special well done must go out to Charlie Fry for scoring five goals in a single match."

Polite applause rippled around the changing room.

The usual cheering and celebrations were still missing.

Barney held up the magic book. He opened the small black book and handed it to Emma to read out to the rest of the team.

In a clear voice, Emma said: "Magpies win. 8-0."

The players murmured with amazement. The book's prediction had been right again. Was it ever going to be wrong?

Barney had not finished.

He took the book from Emma, put it in his tracksuit pocket and indicated for her to sit down.

"It is a pity that such a good team performance has been ruined by a few people who think they are better than the rest."

Charlie's eyes – like the rest of the team – moved to Peter and Annie. Both were looking at the floor.

Barney paused for a second before continuing.

"I never thought I would say this next sentence but … I was ashamed to be manager of Hall Park Magpies Under-13s today."

Barney turned his full attention towards Peter and Annie, who looked like they wanted the ground to open up and swallow them.

He continued: "I have no idea what you two were thinking of.

"Showboating, some would call it.

"It was utterly disrespectful at best, being complete idiots at worst. We never do that.

"We may have been better than them but I can guarantee that they are trying just as hard as any of you."

Barney pulled up the sleeves on his black tracksuit.

He continued: "Remember it was not so long ago that we were getting thrashed every week.

"Imagine if someone had done that to you?

"How would you have felt then?

"There is no place for this mickey-taking show-off nonsense in this team.

"If you don't like it then the door is over there. Leave now."

No-one moved a muscle.

You could hear a pin drop.

"Good. I consider this to be over and done with then.

"Learn the lesson quickly, Magpies, because if it happens again there will be a heavy price to pay."

Barney twirled round and threw Wrecka a big bunch of keys.

"You can lock up tonight, Michael. I have had more than enough excitement for one day."

Then the Magpies manager and his assistant Ted walked out, leaving the speechless team sitting in silence behind them.

9. SECRETS

"That was your fault."

Annie stood over Peter pointing her finger.

Charlie had never seen his friend so mad. She was fuming.

"No, it wasn't! I had to have someone to pass to! Don't try to get out of this one!"

Peter defended himself but Charlie could tell he was behind the football trick that had landed them in such trouble.

When Peter was telling the truth he would be up on his feet, shouting from the rooftops that it was not him.

But he wasn't doing that.

He sat on one of the changing room benches in a huff.

Belly had not looked any of them in the eye since Barney walked out.

They were waiting for Emma to finish getting changed.

They would be the last to leave.

Wrecka was somewhere in the small cubbyhole that Barney called his office as he waited to lock up behind them.

The Magpies team had trickled out one by one since Barney stormed out.

They had barely said a word to each other, just the odd goodbye or a few whispered words here and there.

Once the three of them were alone, Annie had confronted Peter.

Charlie could see nothing was going to get sorted out.

Annie was too angry and Peter was so stubborn that there was no point discussing it any further tonight.

Emma emerged from the girls' part of the changing room. Her blonde hair was scraped back in a plait.

"I just need the toilet and then I'll be with you!" She disappeared into the small loo next to the office.

The lock clicked behind her. They were alone again for a few more moments.

Charlie took a deep breath and decided to play peacemaker. He put his hands out to show he did not want to upset either of them.

"Guys, we are all friends here. Come on, let's not fall out. Things are going so well."

Peter did not react but Annie's temper was out of control. She turned on Charlie with a face like thunder.

"You can keep quiet, Mr Football Genius!

"We weren't all so lucky to get hit by lightning and end up with a magic power! I mean, seriously, you never miss? That's crazy – and really unfair.

"Some of us have to work really hard just to get noticed. You just place an invisible target and score goals!

"We can't all be like you: have everything on a plate. Keep your nose out of my business, Fry!"

Charlie knew Annie was cross with Peter, not him.

She hated Barney being angry with her.

Deep down, she knew the showboating had been out of order. It was completely out of character for her.

Charlie had never fallen out with Annie before – it felt awful.

And her words hurt.

Charlie took a step backwards.

"Annie, I didn't...."

Peter could not stay quiet any longer.

"Annie, you're bang out of order. This is my fault, not Charlie's.

"You think he's lucky? Are you mad?

"He has cystic fibrosis. He got hit by lightning.

"He is always cold. And then the hot days of summer arrive and he gets too hot! He can never win. On top of that, muppets make fun of him because he can't run."

Peter stood up.

He was shorter than Annie but he seemed to grow with every sentence. Charlie had rarely seen his friend so serious.

Peter continued: "Despite all this, Charlie still plays football and tries his best to keep up with the rest of us.

"You are supposed to be one of his best friends but you've got a funny way of showing it."

The toilet flushed and Charlie could hear the taps

running.

Emma would be with them in a moment.

His eyes flashed between the friends. Peter stood, fists clenched and jaw jutted out. He was glaring at Annie intently.

Annie was still red-faced but her bottom lip was wobbling and Charlie thought she might burst into tears.

"All done!" Emma closed the toilet door and marched towards the door.

She seemed to be completely oblivious to the row that was going on among her friends without her.

She yanked open the door and turned to the others: "Come on, let's go home and get some dinner! I'm starving."

Emma did not wait for a response. She took a step outside before stopping quickly.

"Hello Toby!

"What on earth are you doing lurking out here? I thought you had left for home ages ago!"

10. THE LURKER

Charlie's eyes widened with horror. Both Peter and Annie gaped at the doorway where Toby Grace stood in front of them.

They had not been talking too loudly with Emma being so close but Toby could have heard Charlie's secret.

Questions swirled through the Boy Wonder's mind.

How long had Toby been lurking outside the door?

What was he doing there?

Toby stood still and looked at the ground. As usual, a small tuft of brown hair was sticking out at a funny angle.

He was easily the smallest player on the Magpies team but Toby looked even smaller than ever as he stood in the doorway.

Charlie liked Toby.

The Magpies defender was quiet but kind, funny and generous.

Like Charlie, he got a hard time at school.

The usual gang of bullies – it seemed – never gave him a moment's peace unless he was with Charlie, Joe and the rest of the gang.

But now he thought about it ... Toby had been acting differently recently. He had been quieter than normal and seemed stressed out.

Something was wrong.

"Toby?"

Emma raised her eyebrows as she waited for Toby to answer.

Toby's mouth was hidden by a red zip-up tracksuit jacket. When he did finally speak, it came out muffled.

"Er, we can't hear you!"

Slowly Toby undid his top and looked up at Emma.

"I ... have lost my bag. I have searched everywhere ... so I wanted to check if it was still in the changing room."

Peter moved before anyone else.

He walked over to Toby's place in the changing room and picked up a blue rucksack that was hanging on one of the newly painted hooks.

Toby smiled with relief.

"Ah, thank you so much. I have been looking everywhere."

He took the backpack from Peter and put it over his skinny shoulders.

Charlie couldn't help but smile.

Something deep inside told him not to worry – even if Toby knew the big secret.

He was harmless.

They jumped as another voice boomed out behind them.

"Is anybody actually planning to go home tonight

or are we all spending the night here with no dinner?"

Wrecka emerged from the office to find the gang standing in the doorway. He looked at his watch.

"Right, I'm locking up. My dinner is about ready and I'm starving after today's game."

The Magpies captain ushered Charlie, Peter and Annie towards the doorway where Emma and Toby were still standing.

Emma and Charlie followed Toby out of the door with their kitbags.

Annie and Peter followed but stopped when Wrecka grabbed Peter's arm.

"Cut out the showboating in future, you two. We need to concentrate on winning, not fancy flick competitions."

They blushed. The shock of nearly giving away Charlie's secret had made them forget the row they were having.

Peter and Annie nodded and left in silence.

Wrecka was right.

They had been fools.

Emma spoke straight away.

"Come on Annie, my dad is waiting for us and he gets so mad with me for taking so long to get ready."

The girls waved a quick goodbye and began the long walk towards the park's car park area. Charlie noticed Annie did not hug him as she left.

It was the first time that had happened in a long time.

He felt hurt.

Why was he being blamed?

Wrecka finished locking the changing room door and ambled over to join Toby, Peter and Charlie.

"I'm off too. Anyone want a lift home with my

mum?"

They shook their heads. Charlie knew why.

They all wanted to go over the game as they walked home.

It had turned into a ritual – something Charlie, Peter and Toby did after every home match.

Wrecka nodded goodbye and began walking up the sloping footpath, 20 metres or so behind the girls.

The three boys turned in the opposite direction, heading towards the rarely used small gate at the top end of the park.

They had only walked a few steps when Toby grabbed Charlie's arm.

"Charlie. There's something I need to…."

But Toby Grace never managed to finish his sentence.

11. CRASH

"Owwww!"

Charlie cried out as he tumbled to the ground.

He could see that Toby had fallen beside him and was not moving.

Peter lay to his left, clutching his stomach.

Charlie was disorientated and confused. His head hurt where it had hit the concrete path and his lower back throbbed with pain.

What had happened? The screech of brakes above them gave him a clue. Then the horrible, gloating voice confirmed it.

"Well, well, well. We've found three of Crickledon's biggest wimps all together."

Charlie looked towards the sound of the voice.

Adam Knight and his best mate Lee were sitting on their bikes with crazy grins on their faces.

He took a deep breath. The Thrapborough Colts striker had made his life hell for years in primary school.

The shaven-headed thug still went to the same

secondary school but Charlie saw far less of him these days – thankfully.

"Is your bike okay, mate?" Adam asked Lee as the latter inspected his front tyre.

Charlie quickly realised what had happened. The bullies had crashed straight into them from behind. They never heard them coming.

One of the bikes had smashed into Charlie and Toby, sending them flying.

Peter must have turned to see what was attacking them before the second bike ploughed into him, hurting his knee. Both bullies jumped off their bikes.

Lee crouched down and tried to repair the damage while Adam Knight marched over to Toby and ripped his back-pack off.

He then scooped up Peter's kit-bag. He rummaged through that one too before he moved towards the bag Charlie had dropped.

As he came closer, Adam seemed huge. He had always been big – only Joe was a match in size.

Those two had fought more times than Charlie could remember. But Joe was not here and the others could not even begin to stand up.

In desperation, his eyes flicked towards the pathway where Wrecka and the girls had gone. It was empty. They were on their own.

"Get out of our stuff and leave us alone."

Charlie got to his feet and looked directly towards Adam, who was kneeling down with the three bags in front of him.

Lee dropped his bike to the path and stood next to Adam. The bully turned around slowly, an evil smile stuck to his face.

"Look what we have here, Lee. It is Mr Football

Boy Wonder himself. Well, don't worry, Charles.

"I wouldn't be seen dead wearing any of this rubbish."

He threw Peter's kit on to the floor.

Adam flung down the bags and moved in Charlie's direction. The sun sparkled off his cropped hair. He was an intimidating sight.

Charlie's heart was pounding. He was scared but was determined not to let the two bullies see his fear.

"Go away, you pair of morons."

Adam chuckled again. His arm shot out and grabbed Charlie around the neck. The bully's grip was strong and Charlie could not shake him off.

In the background, Lee laughed again.

Adam pulled Charlie closer.

"You are rubbish at football, Fry. This season is a fluke. I'm going to win the golden boot this season. Not you, understand?"

As Charlie considered a reply, he never saw the punch coming. Adam's right hand shot out and pounded deep into his stomach, immediately taking all the air from his body.

Charlie gasped and felt his legs turn to jelly.

It felt like he'd been hit with a shovel. Any fight in him disappeared as quickly as the air left his lungs.

The bigger boy released his grip and Charlie sagged to his knees, heaving for oxygen.

Adam and Lee grabbed their bikes.

"Oh, there's one more thing."

Adam put both feet down on the path and leaned over to whisper in Charlie's ear.

"Don't even think about beating Colts next weekend – or I'll make you pay for it."

12. BULLY

It wasn't even 9am but the morning was sweltering.

School had not started but Charlie could feel his white shirt had become sweaty.

Spring had been boiling so far and today was no different.

Joe, Peter and Charlie sat in their usual spot: a bench outside the school's science block.

The boys had turned up for school early because they had something urgent to discuss – Adam Knight.

"And then they cycled off, laughing their heads off. Once I got my breath back, Toby was on his feet and together we helped Peter get up …."

Charlie's words tailed away.

His story was over.

Peter had his injured leg resting on the bench.

It was very sore but his mum said nothing was broken. He would live, she told him with little sympathy.

Nonetheless Charlie had seen the huge knee

support that was wrapped around his friend's leg.

It looked pretty painful.

Peter could not walk properly at the moment.

He could only hobble along at a snail's pace.

The big game against Thrapborough Colts – and possible revenge against Adam Knight – was only six days away.

Colts were second in the league but they, like Hall Park Rovers, had been stuttering lately.

Adam Knight's goals had dried up in recent weeks and, as a result, the team had struggled to grind out results.

Regardless of their form, Magpies needed Peter if they were going to beat Colts and put pressure on Chell Di Santos's team.

Joe was stroking his chin, deep in thought.

"Did he take anything?"

Peter grimaced as he slid his knee off the bench.

"No, but he bust my leg. He's dead when I catch up with him."

Joe punched his mate playfully on the arm. "You're not catching anyone at the moment, are you Hoppy?"

Charlie cut in before the usual bickering began.

"Why did he rummage through the bags then?"

Peter pulled a face. "No idea. Perhaps it is because he's a nutter?"

"No, it's a good point," Joe replied. "Was he looking for something? And if so, what did he want?"

Charlie shrugged.

He did not know the answer.

The boys sat in silence for a few moments, each thinking about the bully that had plagued them for so long.

It was Joe who spoke again.

"Well, you've got the perfect opportunity for revenge next Saturday. You can do us a huge favour or one for yourselves."

Joe wasn't joking either. Rovers had lost again at the weekend and their lead was now only goal difference.

After their amazing run of form, Magpies were now only two points behind.

It was tight at the top of the Crickledon Under-13s league with the Telegraph describing it as "the most exciting league finale in decades".

Peter piped up again.

"Can you imagine old Chell Di Santos's face if we win the title?

"I can't think of anything I would like to see more. How is the Demon Football Manager doing as his team bottles it?"

"Hey! That's my team too!" Joe shot back hotly but then rolled his eyes.

"He is the same. Wait a minute, no, that's not true.

"He is crazier than ever. He is obsessed with just about everything: timings, food, pitches and even kits.

"You name it. He screams at the players every week. Several of the parents are considering taking their kids away from the mad man."

Charlie looked at Joe. His friend rarely spoke about Rovers these days – and they rarely asked.

Magpies had taken over his life and it had been easy to forget his best mate still played for the division leaders.

"How are you doing there?"

Joe shook his head. "No idea. He doesn't shout at me so I suppose I am in favour.

"We keep letting in careless goals but I usually make enough saves to earn the team a point or three.

"Di Santos never speaks to me. He is too busy trying to goad Bishop."

Brian Bishop was one of the best strikers in the league.

The bruising striker had led the division's goal-scoring charts until Charlie's record-breaking goal glut at the weekend.

Charlie could not understand why the Rovers manager would be nasty to the star striker.

Then he remembered: Chell Di Santos was one of the most unpleasant men he had ever met.

Poor Joe. Poor Bishop.

The school bell went.

Charlie waved the others goodbye as he headed in a different direction.

Saturday would soon be here.

13. BREAKING POINT

"Idiot!"

Chell Di Santos slammed a fist on the table.

The blow forced the keyboard and pen sitting on the desk to jump up into the air.

He said nothing.

All he did was stare.

His cheeks were bright red, which matched his mood.

He was furious.

His quest to uncover Charlie Fry's deepest secrets was going nowhere.

Instead, that annoying Magpies team just kept winning.

Rovers were supposed to be the A-Team – they could not lose the league this season, especially not to Magpies.

His entire career depended on it.

Nobody would gamble on him in England despite his stellar reputation abroad.

Last year he had spent months touting his name

round English football clubs – trying to convince them to take a chance on him.

No-one wanted to know and Di Santos feared he may have to work outside of the game.

Then Hall Park had made contact.

In desperation, he had agreed to take the Rovers' Under-13s manager role.

He planned to use it as a springboard – a year of success would put him on the radar of bigger football clubs.

But Di Santos knew he needed to be a winner.

He had to stop Magpies.

He had to stop Charlie Fry.

Finally the Hall Park Rovers boss spoke.

"Time is running out."

Every word sounded like it had been laced with poison.

A chill went round the room.

The boy sitting opposite went to speak but was silenced by a single, bony finger held in the air.

Di Santos was not finished. Not by a long way.

He stood up.

As usual, he was wearing all black – tie, shirt, trousers and shoes.

Apart from his red cheeks, there was one other sign that revealed Di Santos's terrible rage: a single strand of hair had fallen out of place and he had not corrected it.

"It was a simple thing I asked. Anyone could do it.

"Instead, you have failed."

The icy glare remained.

"You have failed me.

"You have failed yourself.

"You have failed in your bid to be a proper

footballer."

The boy could hold back no longer.

"No! Please! I have nearly discovered his secret!

"Give me until the weekend.

"Please, Mr Di Santos.

"I will do anything.

"Let me prove to you that I can do this, Sir."

The manager glared at the youngster with burning eyes.

He cracked his knuckles loudly as he sat down once more.

Then he fixed his stare back on the terrified boy in front of him and smiled. It was false and scary.

The boy shivered in response.

"You have three days. Do not let me down again.

"This must be done. Charlie Fry must never play football again."

He leaned forward and spoke in a menacing whisper.

"I do not tolerate losers or people who fail. Do you understand?"

The boy nodded eagerly.

Di Santos pushed the stray strand of hair back into place.

"Now get out and get it done."

14. SAVED

The school week seemed to take forever.

Charlie found himself looking at the clock every few minutes. He could not wait for Saturday's big match to arrive.

Eventually the school bell rang on Thursday afternoon. The game against Thrapborough Colts was less than 48 hours away.

Charlie shoved his book and pencil case into his backpack and was the first person to leave class.

Joe and Peter were staying late to train for the school football team but Charlie had decided not to play for the school this year.

He had too many things going on – he couldn't commit to playing for the school as well. It was one of those things.

He needed rest as well as exercise.

And it was Magpies who had his full attention.

Charlie had decided his plan: get home as quickly as possible, do some physio, wolf down some dinner and then practise free-kicks against his little brother

Harry in their back garden.

He raced out of the classroom and leapt down the stairs three at a time.

Within seconds, he was outside and heading towards the school gates.

Only a couple of other kids had been quicker to leave lessons than him so the wide pathway was empty.

Within a minute or two, it would be packed by chatting schoolkids beginning their walk home.

Charlie paused for a second and spun around.

He had heard something.

It sounded like a cry for help.

"Arrgghh! Gerrrooff!"

Charlie knew that voice anywhere. It was Toby.

Thoughts of leaving early disappeared.

Instead of heading to the gate, Charlie took a right-hand turn and headed towards the science block.

As he turned the corner, Charlie's eyes widened.

A couple of older boys, who were probably about 14, had Toby pinned up against the wall.

They were big – and towered over both Toby and Charlie.

Still, he could not let his friend get beaten up by those two idiots.

"Leave him alone."

Charlie managed to keep his voice steady but inside his stomach was tight and anxious. He hated fighting.

The biggest thug turned to meet the newcomer. He seemed to be huge, as big as most of the adults Charlie knew.

The bully began to approach him.

He had long brown hair, parted in the middle like a pair of curtains. He had several spots on the end of his big nose.

The teenager spat chewing gum in Charlie's direction before a grin broke out across his smug face.

"Get lost, wimp. This doesn't involve you."

"Help me, Charlie!" Toby whimpered as the other thug kept him pinned to the wall with a forearm across his throat.

Toby's nose was bleeding. Charlie had to do something.

"No, that is where you're wrong. He is my friend and you're hurting him. Put him down and go away. I don't want any trouble."

The older boy stepped closer.

"Well, that's not your choice is it?"

The thug was almost on top of him. He stank of cheap deodorant.

A massive hand shot out and grabbed Charlie round the back of the neck.

Before Charlie could react, he was swept off the ground by the older boy and dangled helplessly above the ground.

"It looks like this little hero isn't going to be your saviour after all, wimp boy."

Charlie squirmed and kicked his legs wildly but it was no use. The thug was too strong for him.

"Wait."

The boy holding Toby against the wall was looking intently at Charlie.

"I know you. You're …"

Toby finished the sentence.

"... Charlie Fry. Yes, you idiots are trying to bully

the Football Boy Wonder – Crickledon's best ever football player."

Charlie could see the older boy's eyes widening with horror as he realised what was happening.

A second later, he dropped Toby, who fell into a heap on the floor.

"Put him down, Pittan. It's time to go."

His friend looked amazed. He did not put Charlie down either.

"What? No way. This shrimp needs to be taught a lesson."

Charlie saw the thug's hand close into a fist and prepared for the punch.

It never arrived.

The friend caught Pittan's arm as he pulled it back to strike Charlie.

Shocked, he dropped Charlie, who scrambled away towards Toby.

"What are you doing?" Pittan looked mad.

His friend, though, was already on the move, headed towards the school gate.

"If we touch the Boy Wonder, everyone will be after us … and I mean everyone. It is far too much trouble, even for me."

Red-faced and still arguing, Pittan slowly followed his friend towards the gates.

Their voices were soon lost in the background noise as hundreds of kids began leaving the school.

Charlie helped Toby to his feet.

"Are you okay?"

Toby nodded as he fished a tissue out of his pocket to wipe his bleeding nose.

"What did they want?"

Toby shook his head. "No idea. I was trying to get

out early for once and those two gorillas grabbed me as I walked past."

Charlie chuckled. "You're being unfair on gorillas. They're far cleverer than that Pittan bloke!"

The friends laughed together and began slowly walking towards the gate.

By now, there were people everywhere. There was no chance the bullies would be back now.

A thought sprung into Charlie's mind.

"I've been messaging you, Toby, but haven't had an answer? Is everything okay?"

Toby looked fed up. "My phone's gone missing. No idea when I lost it. Sorry buddy, I haven't been ignoring you on purpose.

"My mum is taking me to get a new phone though so I'll be back online really soon."

They reached the gate and prepared to head different ways.

Toby's mum was picking him up from the car park.

"Ah, cool. I thought we'd fallen out without me knowing why! Hope you get it sorted out soon. We need everyone focused on Saturday!"

Toby nodded eagerly. "Don't worry about that, Boy Wonder! I can't wait!"

He turned to go but took a couple of paces and stopped.

"Charlie?"

Charlie turned back to face his friend again.

"Yes, Toby?"

"Thanks."

15. DANGER

"Charlie! Can you get the door please?"

Charlie pulled himself off the sofa and slouched towards the door.

The Football Boy Wonder had finished doing his daily physio about half an hour ago but was still lazing in front of the telly.

He thought his mum hadn't noticed – but she had, of course. Like most mums, very little got past Molly Fry.

Still Charlie felt great.

His chest was clear and the routine of matches, training and practising was helping it remain that way. Eating was even okay.

He pulled open the door with a huge smile … and then he did not know what to say.

It was Annie.

They still hadn't spoken since the argument nearly a week ago.

And now she was standing on his doorstep.

"Er … hi."

Annie sounded nervous, which was so unusual for her.

"Hi," he replied awkwardly and began to look at the floor. He tapped the carpet with one of his toes.

There was an awkward silence before Annie spoke again.

"Look, Charlie. I ... am sorry ... for what I said last week.

"It was completely out of order. I was so mad with myself and Peter ... and I took it out on you.

"That was really unfair. I am so sorry."

The words came out quickly as if Annie had been rehearsing them beforehand.

Charlie beamed.

He had his friend back.

"Annie. Don't ignore me if you're mad – come and talk to me about it."

Annie grinned with relief.

"I know, I know.

"But I felt so angry. Then I calmed down and became so embarrassed over what had happened and didn't know how to tell you.

"And then I saw what you did for Toby and I knew we had to make up."

Charlie scratched above his ear.

"You saw that?!"

Charlie did not think anyone had seen him coming to Toby's aid the day before. He had been wrong, it seemed.

Annie nodded. "Yes, I came around the corner as you stepped into the fight.

"Toby is very lucky to have such a good friend ... and so am I."

Annie was unable to stop the tears this time.

Charlie grinned again.

"Forget about last week. I have done already."

"Really?"

Charlie laughed. "Of course! Do you fancy practising headers? Harry will be the keeper for us. We need to train for tomorrow!"

Annie stepped into the house. Charlie closed the door behind her and guided Annie through the house into the back garden.

As they passed through the kitchen, Charlie heard his phone buzz with a message.

"Harry, this is Annie. You know, one of the girls from Magpies. Can you look after her please, while I grab my phone?"

Ball under his arm, Harry was there in a flash.

"So is your dad really Johnny Cooper?!"

Annie laughed at the question she had been asked a thousand times.

"Yep, he's my dad – but he's not as good as me!"

She knocked the ball out from under Harry's arm and raced towards the goal at the far end of the garden.

Charlie chuckled as he walked back into the house.

He grabbed the phone from the kitchen counter.

A quick flick of his thumb-print unlocked the smartphone and the message flashed up on the screen.

It had been sent by an unknown number, someone that Charlie did not have saved in his phone.

He gasped.

The message sent a chill down his spine.

Two words looked back at him.

"I know."

16. LIES

The words hovered in front of Charlie's face.

He blinked and looked again. They remained the same. Charlie suddenly felt sick.

He slumped down on one of the kitchen table chairs and re-read the text message.

"I know."

Charlie's thumbs flew over the keypad.

He typed: "Who are you?" before hitting the send button in panic.

He looked at the screen intently.

No response.

What was this person talking about?

They surely weren't talking about his big secret, were they?

Only a handful of people knew – and Charlie would trust them with his life.

None of his friends would tell.

Surely they must be talking about something else?

Charlie looked at the number again.

It was no use. It was just a bunch of numbers

floating in front of his eyes with no name attached to it.

But he only had a few friends stored in his phone: Joe, Peter, Mudder, and Wrecka. He didn't even have Annie's number.

"Come on," Charlie mumbled out loud as his hand remained gripped tightly around the smartphone.

"Er ... are you talking to me, Mr Fry?"

Annie's voice piped up behind Charlie. She giggled as he jumped with surprise, completely unaware of the situation.

Charlie blushed. How could he explain this one?

"Er ... ha ... no. I ...."

He could hear his own voice tail off as he struggled to find the right words.

Annie, however, did not seem to notice.

She chuckled at Charlie's dithering and plonked herself down next to her friend.

"Come on, dipstick," she said with a smile.

"Your little brother is running rings around me out there ... I need some help before he gets even further ahead!"

Charlie forced himself to smile.

Annie put a hand on his shoulder.

"Seriously, he is too good for me to beat on my own.

"Luckily, I know a certain Boy Wonder who may want to help me out!"

She laughed at her joke and jumped up.

Annie continued: "Besides we need to get every bit of practise we can get if we are going to beat Adam Knight's mob tomorrow."

Charlie gritted his teeth at the mention of Adam. He could not remember wanting to win a game as much as this one.

Apart from Chell Di Santos, he wanted to beat Adam Knight more than anyone.

Annie was right, as usual.

They moved out of the kitchen and through the back door into the garden to find Harry impatiently waiting for the game to restart.

"At last! Where have you been?"

Harry did not wait for an answer from his older brother as he placed the ball carefully on the halfway line in their garden.

"It is 11-5 to me!"

Charlie and Annie laughed together at Harry's enthusiasm for football.

Seconds later, there was a loud bang.

"12-5 … to me!"

Harry squealed with joy as the right-footed shot flew into the small gap between Annie and Charlie.

The ball hit the fence, making a crack in the wood.

The boys knew what was coming. Seconds later, a voice boomed out of the bedroom window.

"WHO DID THAT?! I have told you boys so many times! Leave that fence alone! Don't make me ban ball games in the garden again!"

Charlie and Harry both winced. Football in the back garden always made their mother mad.

"Yes, mum!" They replied together as the window slammed shut above them.

With all the commotion, Charlie had completely forgotten his phone and the threatening message.

It was sitting where he left it – alone on the kitchen table.

And no-one heard the phone beep as the next message arrived.

17. MIND GAMES

The ball bounced against the wall and crashed into the light above the changing room's row of pegs.

Peter winced and looked in the direction of Barney's office.

He was prepared for the Magpies manager to fly into the changing room and tell them off for wrecking the place.

Barney though did not appear and Peter breathed a huge sigh of relief.

He had got away with it. He smiled nervously at Charlie and Annie and scooped the ball up to stop it escaping again.

It was 1pm.

Barney and the team's physio Ted had been shocked to see the three of them turn up a whole hour before kick-off but they could not wait any longer.

The rest of the Magpies hadn't arrived yet.

While the management team talked tactics in the office, Charlie had told Annie and Peter about the mysterious text messages.

Peter pursed his lips.

"So Fry, tell me again. What did it say? I need to know … exactly."

Charlie tutted. They had been through this already.

"I told you.

"The first one said 'I know' and, when I asked them what they were talking about, they said: 'Confess everything and your secret will be safe with me.'

"I didn't reply again. That's it."

Peter rubbed his jaw. "Hmmmm. This is a tricky one."

"Well done, Sherlock. I could have told you that," replied Charlie sarcastically.

Peter punched his friend's knee in response.

"Okay, Mr Grumpy. I am trying to help. Do you think they know?

"You know, about the magic target and how it works?"

Annie had not said a word until now.

"How could they know? The target is inside Charlie's head. No-one else can see it. And only your best friends know.

"Whoever it is, they're trying to trick you into confessing."

She spoke in a whisper. Her voice died off and the boys did not reply.

Finally Peter broke the silence.

"Well, block the number and forget about it.

"Your secret is safe.

"Let's get hold of Joe; vow to never speak about it again and no-one can ever prove anything. It is really simple."

Charlie coughed and clutched his left lung as a jolt of pain shot through it.

Annie put her hand on his shoulder.

"You okay, Boy Wonder? You look shattered."

He smiled.

"I am fine. I didn't get much sleep last night but I like Peter's plan. Don't worry about me – let's worry about smashing Colts instead."

Seconds later, Annie looked up with her eyes burning brightly.

"So you phone doesn't recognise the number?"

Charlie broke away to look at his friend.

"No ... but I haven't got many numbers."

"What is it?"

Charlie rummaged in his coat pocket and pulled out the phone. He held up the message with the mysterious phone number on it.

Annie and Peter began to scroll through their contacts in their phones. After a few moments, both of them shook their heads.

Neither of them knew who had sent the message either.

Annie scratched her head. "Hang on, we're being really stupid. Have you even tried ringing the number?"

Charlie went red. It had never even occurred to him.

"No ..." Charlie began to explain.

The changing room door flung open. It was Wrecka.

"COME ON MAGPIES!"

The captain bounced into the room unaware that he was interrupting an important conversation.

Toby trailed in behind him.

Wrecka turned and flung an arm around the smaller boy. "It seems like Toby was too scared to come in alone! I found him outside the door waiting for me!"

Peter flashed a look at Charlie and Annie.

What had Toby been doing outside?

Before any of them could speak, the changing room slammed open again causing them all to jump.

Adam Knight, complete with freshly shaven head, stood in the doorway.

"Look at the losers having a little party. You won't be so happy in a couple of hours' time, you bunch of muppets."

He spat on the floor and laughed wickedly.

Wrecka moved before anyone else.

Within three strides he had reached the gloating Colts player and pushed him straight back out of the door.

As Adam fell backwards, Wrecka ensured he was fully out of the changing room – and slammed the door in his face without another word.

The Magpies captain rubbed his hands together as he looked around at his friends.

"We can't let him win today. No way."

18. NERVES

Manor Park had never been so full.

Charlie had seen the crowds steadily swell as Magpies had begun the winning streak that had shot them up the table.

Barely 30 people had been watching when Charlie had made his first start for Barney's team.

The trickle of people had become a flood in recent weeks – with more than 200 turning out for their last victory on home turf.

Yet this was ridiculous.

Barney estimated 1,000 people were waiting for today's game to begin.

Coops thought the attendance was closer to 2,000. Charlie did not know who was right but either way, a lot of people waited outside.

They were everywhere.

Manor Park did not have stands like Hall Park's main stadium.

It was simply a normal park with a football pitch in the middle, a couple of rickety changing rooms and some beaten-up play equipment.

But today people were crammed around the pitch.

Kids had climbed to the top of the climbing frame to watch while others had scrambled up trees to get a better view.

Hall Park Magpies Under-13s v Thrapborough Colts Under-13s.

It was a six-pointer: second versus third with both teams desperate to clinch one of the two promotion places on offer.

This was the game they had been waiting for.

Charlie forced the mysterious text messages out of his mind. There would be plenty of time to worry about them later.

Instead, he remembered all the taunts he had endured from Adam Knight.

For years, he had tried to be the bully's friend but it had never worked.

Adam would never accept him – he was too different, 'not normal' enough in the bully's eyes.

In the past year, though, Charlie had given up trying to be nice. He just wanted to shut Adam up once and for all.

And the best way to do that was on the pitch.

The Football Boy Wonder felt the butterflies in his stomach as he peered out of the changing room window towards the pitch.

"Charlie?"

He turned and realised the entire changing room was looking in his direction.

"Have you been listening to anything I've been saying?"

Barney stood in the centre of the room.

Charlie knew there was no point in lying.

He held up his hands: "I'm sorry, boss. I just can't take my mind off the crowd, the pitch ..."

His voice tailed off. Charlie felt his stomach lurch with nerves again.

"I'm sorry."

Barney chuckled.

The unexpected laugh lifted the tension in the room immediately.

"What are you sorry for, sunshine? If everyone is as focused as you then I see little point in a team talk."

The Magpies boss pinned the team sheet up in its usual place and turned to face the team again.

He snapped: "Here's the team.

"I'm off to speak to the ref about making sure this crowd is safe.

"Get those boots done up. We will do the warm-up in five minutes."

Wrecka spoke up for the rest of the team. "What's the book's prediction, gaffer?"

Barney paused and his face turned a shade of red. Something was wrong.

"I ... well ... there's been a slight problem with the magic book."

Barney could not find the right words.

"I'm sorry. We seem to have lost the book."

There was a gasp from the whole team.

Barney held out his hands. "Coops is looking for it as we speak but I really don't think it matters. We are going to win, no matter what happens. I can feel it in the air."

No-one responded so Barney headed towards the door.

As he left, the team surged towards the team sheet

to see who would be playing in the biggest match in the Magpies' short history.

Charlie watched the faces of his teammates as they saw the team.

People liked Peter and Greavesy were bouncing off the ceiling as they saw their names in the line-up.

Charlie could see others were concerned about the book's disappearance. Billy Savage had his head in his hands.

Annie was looking around the room as if trying to find it.

And a couple of people had sat back down. Even Charlie's own stomach had dropped and he suddenly felt a bit sick.

There were a few of the players muttering between themselves – no doubt talking about the missing book that had been so lucky for them in recent weeks.

Everyone seemed to be nervous – Toby in particular looked terrified.

As if echoing Charlie's own thoughts, Toby asked out loud: "What if the magic book says we're going to lose?"

"We better just keep our fingers crossed that it doesn't!" replied Wrecka quietly, staring straight ahead.

The Boy Wonder was the last person to go up to the team-sheet. Charlie was confident he would be in the team – and he was right.

Hall Park Magpies Under-13s v Thrapborough Colts Under-13s

Saturday, April 2
Manor Park

Manager: Barney Payne

1. Darren Bunnell
2. Billy Savage
3. Toby Grace
4. Wrecka (c)
5. Annie Cooper
6. Theo Tennison
7. Paul Greaves
8. Charlie Fry
9. Emma Tysoe
10. Paul Flemmell
11. Peter Bell

Subs: Jimmy Welford, Gary Bradshaw.

Charlie felt an arm around his neck as he gazed at the team-sheet.

"You can do it," Annie whispered. "We're going smash this lot and then find out who sent that message. Trust me."

Charlie gave Annie a quick smile as she headed back towards the girls' part of the changing room and he returned to his seat next to Toby.

He had pulled on one of his boots when Barney came back.

He marched into the room with a bright red face and ruffled hair. He looked around, surprised there wasn't more noise from the team.

"Right, I've spoken to the ref. We need to get this game under way before this crowd gets any bigger.

"We've managed to find some volunteers and they're going to sit around the pitch to make sure no-one goes on it – apart from the players, of course."

At that moment Charlie realised Barney was nervous too. A huge crowd, a big game – even older people can get nerves.

Barney moved to the door before he faced the team again.

"I can tell you are ready, Magpies.

"I will tell you this: I have never managed such an amazing team in all my years in football. Some games we need tactics and rousing speeches.

"Today is not one of those days. You know what to do. You know how we play. We dig in, help each other and never, ever give up.

"Forget about the book. We will win today – because we want it more. I promise you that.

"Now Wrecka lead us out – and get that win."

19. THE BIG MATCH

It was hard to believe the level of noise generated by the crowd.

It felt like being plunged into a cauldron of sound.

In their immaculate green shirts, yellow shorts and green socks, the Magpies team lined up proudly as they waited for Colts.

The Boy Wonder was at the end of the line. He could see his family, standing on the opposite touchline near the halfway line.

Harry was perched upon his dad's shoulders and waved like mad.

Charlie could not see his mum but knew she was there somewhere. He gave Harry a thumbs-up and saw the younger boy smiled with delight.

Charlie took a quick glimpse down the line at his teammates.

Every single one of them looked ahead, their concentration was complete. He had never seen Magpies looked so determined.

The warm-up was finished.

Now they stood and waited for Colts, who had returned to the changing room, to reappear.

The wait was not long.

Led by Adam Knight, the Colts ran out in a flash of red and white.

One end of the Manor Park crowd burst out into applause at the sight of the Colts players.

The away end, Charlie guessed, as a few flags came out. In all of their previous matches, all the fans had mixed together.

Today there were too many for that.

The Colts players began moving down the Magpies line, shaking hands as they went.

Charlie swallowed to try to shake off the nerves. Shaking hands with Adam Knight was something he had been dreading.

Charlie watched as the bully approached.

After brief handshakes with the referee and two linesmen, Adam Knight stepped up to Wrecka with his hand outstretched.

As Wrecka accepted the handshake, Adam pulled him closer and pretended to eyeball the opposition captain.

While he did this, Adam craftily stamped on Wrecka's foot.

No-one noticed, apart from Charlie.

Wrecka did not make a fuss about the wind-up.

He winced with pain, gently pushed Adam away and stuck out his hand towards the next player in the line.

Adam grinned and swaggered towards the next player in the line – getting closer towards the Boy Wonder.

Peter did not even attempt to shake hands with the

bully. He kept looking along the line and Adam did exactly the same in the opposite direction.

Emma and Annie barely touched the Colts striker's hand.

As he got closer, Charlie realised Adam was making a strange sound as he passed the Magpies players.

He seemed to be growling.

Despite his nervousness, Charlie stifled a giggle.

Growling? Was he some kind of dog?

Finally the moment arrived. For a second Charlie also considered refusing to shake hands with his enemy.

But he would not let Adam Knight intimidate him.

Instead he took a deep breath and thrust his hand out.

The bully grabbed it and squeezed with such force that Charlie feared his bones may be crushed.

The Boy Wonder did not cry out.

He would not give Adam the satisfaction.

Eventually Adam released his grip but crashed his shoulder into Charlie's chest on purpose as he turned to run towards the other end of the pitch.

The next handshake was the same for Charlie.

Almost every member of the Colts team tried to break his fingers.

After the first four players, Charlie could no longer feel his hand. But he never stopped looking them in the eye.

He knew they wanted to frighten him. They wanted to put him off his game and break his concentration.

No chance.

Only one player was different.

The final player walking down the line of handshakes was a huge boy who looked as if he was ready for bed.

Charlie had never met him before but the legend of Stephen Cleatman was well known throughout Crickledon.

Adam Knight may have scored all the goals for Colts but Cleatman was the football brains behind the team.

He dwarfed everyone else on the pitch but it was his immaculate first touch and ability to see a pass that set him apart.

Hall Park Rovers had been desperate to sign him in the summer but had somehow missed out.

It turned out Cleatman was a fine musician and wanted to continue playing in a band as well as playing football every week.

However Chell Di Santos insisted he must concentrate only on football or he could not play for them.

Cleatman was not the type to be bullied. He loved his music so he turned Rovers down and turned out instead for Colts, who could barely believe their luck.

It was a mistake to let him go. He had been one of the league's star performers – and had created more goals than anyone else.

Now he stood in front of the Boy Wonder with his red socks already rolled down to his ankles.

With his hand out in front of him, Charlie waited for the bone-crunching to begin.

Yet he was mistaken. Cleatman returned the handshake with a firm grip but nothing more.

He pushed a bucket-sized hand through his shaggy light brown hair and smiled at Charlie's look of surprise.

"May the best man win, Boy Wonder. Let's do it."

He gave Charlie a friendly thump on the back before racing off to join the rest of the Colts team.

Charlie didn't have time to dwell on the strange encounter. Wrecka was signalling for a team huddle before kick-off.

The big match had finally arrived.

20. SPECIAL ONE

Stephen Cleatman was the real deal.

Within minutes of the game starting, Charlie knew they were playing against someone who had magic in their boots.

His passing was superb. He sprayed the ball around the Manor Park pitch at will and left Magpies chasing shadows.

The problem was simple: the Magpies midfielders were getting swamped.

Theo was having a fine game but Greavesy was struggling. He was battling hard but he could not get near Cleatman.

The Colts midfielder looked like he had all the time in the world despite Greavesy's constant attentions.

The real problem was Flem.

Magpies' first choice midfielder Gary Bradshaw had been struggling to sleep, complaining about regular nightmares of scoring own goals.

Barney decided Bradshaw's lack of sleep meant he

was only fit enough for the bench.

So Flem had been given the nod instead.

It did not begin well.

Adam Knight had cackled loudly as the hapless Flem was nutmegged in the first minute.

It had been a bad start and things had gone downhill from there. While Cleatman seemed to float over the pitch, Flem looked like he was running in treacle.

His face was red and his fancy haircut was mangled with sweat. Flem was trying his best but he could not cope.

It was like Magpies were playing with ten men.

None of the Magpies frontline had got hold of the ball yet.

Peter and Emma had been dragged back to help the midfield, leaving Charlie alone up front and completely outnumbered.

The pressure from Colts was intense.

Finally Cleatman made a mistake. The midfielder had waltzed past Flem but did not see Greavesy slide in on his blind side.

Realising his mistake too late, Cleatman tried to save the attack with a through ball but rushed it.

He over-hit the pass and saw the ball harmlessly bobble through to Mudder.

More than half the Colts team had surged up the pitch and it provided the opportunity that Magpies had been waiting for.

Without a second glance, Mudder launched the ball in Charlie's direction.

He knew where the Boy Wonder would be. He did not need to look.

Charlie was already moving.

The Magpies goalkeeper knew to throw the ball over him and the last defenders, forcing them to turn and run towards their own goal.

And as Charlie always knew where the ball was going, he had a head start. They worked on it endlessly in training – and it paid off.

Charlie watched the ball carefully as he began to accelerate behind the Colts' backline.

Then ... BANG!

Charlie was not sure what had happened. One moment he was racing towards the ball; the next he was looking at the sky, flat on his back.

A face peered over him.

Chapman Blooker, the Colts centre-back, sneered: "Not so special."

In a flash he was gone.

Charlie sat up and gasped for breath.

The game was still going on as he sat on the ground.

The referee had obviously not seen a foul and let the play continue.

"Keep going Charlie," bellowed Barney from the touchline.

Blinder was a few feet away, keeping an eye on Charlie as the Boy Wonder slowly got to his feet.

Charlie knew the burly defender had tripped him on purpose yet had somehow got away with it.

Perhaps he practised cheating, Charlie thought as he jogged towards the left wing to put some space between him and Blooker.

Once more, the action was back in the Magpies half with Cleatman in the thick of things again.

His curling shot from outside the box took a wicked deflection off Toby's outstretched foot and flew towards the Magpies goal.

Charlie's heart sank as he saw the ball hurtle towards the net and knew it was the first goal of the game.

Yet the net did not ripple as Charlie had anticipated. At the last moment, Mudder flung himself towards the ball.

The merest touch was enough.

Mudder's fingertips diverted the ball up and over the crossbar.

The home crowd exploded with relief while everyone in the Colts end groaned with disbelief. They sensed how important the first goal in this game would be.

Charlie blew out his cheeks.

A corner was a much better outcome than a goal – and they might get a chance to break away if they defended properly.

Cleatman took the corner – a vicious in-swinger that dipped quickly inside the penalty area.

For once Wrecka misjudged the flight of the ball and there was Blooker to head the ball past a helpless Mudder.

GOAL! 1-0 to Colts.

The crowd at the far end of the pitch let out a huge roar as the ball hit the back of the net.

Blooker pumped his fist towards the silent home fans and high-fived the rest of the Colts team as they began heading back to the half-way line for the restart.

The beefy defender winked at Charlie and smiled.

Both teams knew how important the first goal was.

And the opening goal had gone to Colts.

21. SEEING RED

"Come on Magpies! Let's get moving and get in this game!"

Dripping with sweat, Wrecka bellowed at the rest of the dejected Magpies team as they lined up for the restart.

No-one replied.

Even Peter was silent.

He did not look at Charlie as they got the game going again.

Colts were too good.

No, that wasn't true.

Cleatman was too good.

But it wasn't only him.

Something else was missing. The confidence that had oozed out of Magpies in recent weeks had disappeared.

It was like they had gone backwards. They were like the team at the bottom of the table again, struggling to compete with other teams.

Charlie knew what Peter and the others were

thinking: they needed the book.

It was too late now though.

Within seconds, Colts won the ball again and had pushed Magpies back towards their own area.

Pass, pass, and pass.

The combinations from Colts were making Charlie feel dizzy.

And then Adam Knight hit it from a couple of metres outside the penalty box.

The shot started low as it flew past Annie's despairing lunge before rising wickedly. Yet again Mudder was there.

Somehow the big keeper flung himself to his right and his big palm turned the ball over for a corner kick.

"COME ON MAGPIES! WHAT'S GOING ON?"

Mudder roared with anger as the crowd applauded his excellent goalkeeping. He was keeping Colts at bay almost on his own at the moment.

But the danger wasn't over.

Cleatman whipped in the corner with real fizz, beating Toby on the front post before dipping in the centre of the goal.

Blooker and Adam were waiting, queuing up to grab the goal that would probably put the game out of Magpies' reach.

The ball never arrived though.

Out of nowhere, Annie leapt above the Colts players and headed the ball out of the penalty area.

Magpies always left Charlie up the pitch in case they got the chance for a counter attack.

Even before he had started to move, Emma was screaming at him as she burst forward ahead of the others.

"To me, Charlie!"

As Charlie moved towards the ball, he knew Emma would move into the space he had created behind him.

But the Colts defender had spotted the danger too and reached the ball at the exact same moment as the Boy Wonder.

As Charlie tried to bring the ball under control, the full-back went straight through the back of his leg.

"Arrghhh!"

Charlie cried out as pain shot through his thigh. He fell to the floor and clutched his right leg in agony.

The Colts player did not say a word. He picked himself up, dusted down his shirt and began moving back towards his own goal.

The ref was whistled for a throw-in to Colts and indicated the final touch had been Charlie's.

"REF! Are you KIDDING ME? That's a foul!"

Charlie had never heard Emma sound so mad.

"And you're a cheat!"

Charlie watched the Colts defender simply smirk in response and move further away from Emma.

Instead the Magpies winger turned her attention back to the ref, a grey-haired, kind chap called Nigel.

"This is the worst decision I have ever seen."

Emma was usually ice cool.

Today she was like a volcano waiting to erupt.

"No, it was a fair tackle, young lady. And we'll have a little less of that tone please.

"Now move back so the physio can help your friend here."

Ted jogged on to the pitch and helped move Charlie a metre towards the touchline.

Emma could not hide the anger in her eyes.

After what seemed like an age, she turned away from Charlie but was still muttering loudly to herself as she moved away.

Charlie could not hear what Emma said. But the referee did. He twirled in an instant and marched towards her.

"We certainly do not need language like that," said Nigel rather stiffly.

He flourished a yellow card above Emma's head and began to write down her name and number on the card.

Emma threw up her hands in protest: "But ref…."

Nigel put up a hand to indicate the conversation was over.

Peter jogged over and began to pull Emma away. She was still shaking her head when Colts took the throw-in.

In a flash they were heading towards the Magpies penalty area again.

They were only stopped when Billy Savage threw himself in front of a cross to put it behind for a corner.

"Ouch!"

Ted had the magic sponge on Charlie's thigh but it was not helping. The Boy Wonder could no longer feel his leg.

The Magpies physio shook his head.

"Charlie, you've a dead leg. I can use some spray but there's not much more I can do. Can you stand?"

Charlie did not know if he could or not. Despair was beginning to creep into his stomach – his big game could be over.

"Yes … I think so."

Ted frowned. "Ok, look it is nearly half-time. I'll work on your leg through the break and let's see how you go in the second half."

Charlie's heart leapt. He still had a chance.

"Thanks Ted."

The physio did not respond. His eyes were glued to the other end of the pitch. Charlie followed his gaze.

Something was happening in the middle of the Magpies goalmouth.

Adam Knight was curled into a ball as players from both sides argued about what had happened.

Charlie was confused. He had not seen anything because he had been talking to Ted.

Yet the Colts players were livid.

The ref's whistle calmed the chaos.

Nigel stood over Adam, who was still writhing on the ground.

Aware that every person in the crowd was watching him, the referee pointed directly at the penalty spot.

The Colts supporters burst into cheers as a grim silence hung over the Magpies fans.

But Nigel was not finished.

He turned back to the players and produced a red card, pointing at the person who would play no further part in the match.

Charlie's eyes grew wide as he saw the player begin to make the lonely march back to the changing rooms for an early bath.

Emma had been sent off.

22. THE TRUTH

"What happened?"

With the help of Ted, Charlie had limped to the far side of the pitch to join the rest of Magpies for half-time.

Both Barney and Coops had gone to see Emma so, for a moment, the team sat around sipping from water bottles. They looked battered and bruised.

They finished the first half 2-0 down. Charlie had watched helplessly as Adam had sent Mudder the wrong way from the penalty spot.

No-one responded to Charlie's question.

The Boy Wonder remained standing with his hands on hips. He feared his injured leg wouldn't allow him to get up again if he sat down.

"Er ... hello?"

Peter puffed out his cheeks.

"It all happened so quickly. We were getting ready for the corner when Adam Knight stamped on Wrecka's foot."

Charlie's eyes flicked to his captain. Wrecka's boot

was off and his green sock had turned black with blood.

He did not make a fuss but Charlie knew he was hurting. The grim look on Wrecka's face said it all.

Peter continued: "He was sneaky. No-one saw it. Wrecka did not react or do anything ... so Adam did it again.

"Once more, the ref and linesman missed it. And that's when Emma lost it.

"She pushed Adam in the back – hard. When he turned around, she kicked him in the ... privates."

Charlie winced along with a couple of the other boys.

Annie piped up: "He deserved it!"

Most of the team nodded. Wrecka shook his head as he tried to ram his boot back on his injured foot.

"Right or wrong, it doesn't matter now. We are losing by two goals and only have ten men. We have let ourselves down so far."

A murmur of agreement went around the team again.

"Well said, skipper." A familiar voice boomed out from behind Charlie.

Coops strode into the centre of the circle.

"Er, where's Barney?" Flem asked.

Coops twirled around. "He is looking after Emma. She's pretty upset but that is not our concern at the moment. We have a football game to save. Now why have we forgotten to turn up today?"

The excuses came thick and fast.

"They are too quick."

"They are too strong."

"Cleatman is sick."

Coops sighed.

"Ok. Someone tell me what is really wrong?"

Silence. Then Toby answered in the smallest voice possible.

"It's the book. We need it … and it has been lost."

To everyone's amazement, Coops laughed loudly.

He dug into the back pocket of his skinny jeans and pulled out the familiar black notebook.

"Do you mean this?

A gasp went round the team. They still had the magic book.

Coops waved the book in front of them.

"You lot are complete idiots."

Charlie looked at Mudder in confusion. He could see the goalkeeper looking equally puzzled along with the others.

"This book is not magic. It never has been.

"I write down the scores and you made them happen because you believed in it so much.

"Sometimes I reckon you could have scored even more – but you didn't want to prove the book wrong. It has all been a farce."

Peter jumped up with his fist in the air: "Yes, I knew it!"

Coops nodded. "Yes, Mr Bell never quite believed me but most of you did. And that was enough."

"But why?" Toby's voice quivered as he spoke. He looked close to tears.

Coops tone softened. He dropped down to the level of the most of the team, squatting on his powerful legs.

"The answer is simple.

"The magic to win doesn't come from within this book. It comes from you.

"You were so used to losing every match that you

were beaten before we had even kicked off.

"It was a trick, a rubbish trick, but it worked.

"The book gave you the belief that was missing before. And it changed you into the team of winners that are sitting before me.

"The book has been magic but not in the way you think. It has transformed you and, as a result, you have outgrown all this nonsense."

And with one quick movement, Coops tore the magic football book in two before the team's eyes.

Billy Savage gasped with horror. Gary Bradshaw's eyes widened with shock.

Coops dumped the useless remains of the book on the floor.

"You are winners. You are the best in this league, by a mile, and you don't need a silly book to win games."

Coops paused to let the words sink in.

Several of the team could not take their eyes off the remains of the magic book, fluttering uselessly in the breeze.

A small, high-pitched voice could be heard from the sideline.

"Come on Charlie! Come on Annie! Come on Belly! We can still thrash this lot. Let's score five this half!"

Harry Fry was shouting at the top of his voice as he sat perched around his dad's shoulders.

Coops smiled and addressed the team again.

"Harry believes in you.

"I believe in you.

"But the only question that truly matters is this one: do *you* believe, Magpies?"

23. SWITCH

"Belly, I can't run."

Charlie was hobbling towards the centre circle alongside Peter.

"I know that. I have known you forever."

Charlie shook his head. "No, it isn't my lungs. It's my leg. I can barely move it."

It was typical Peter. He had not even realised his friend was struggling.

"What?! Why didn't you tell Coops? Do you need to come off?"

Charlie could see Colts beginning to take their positions in the other half. He was impressed with them – there was no sign of early celebrations like other teams.

Instead there was just a cold determination to get the win that would virtually seal their promotion.

Charlie turned back to Peter. "Look, I can still play – you are going to need me. You go up front and I'll drop back into the midfield. Flem can support you."

Peter rolled his eyes but still slapped Charlie on the

back. "No problem, sicknote."

Peter called over Flem, Theo and Greavesy into a quick huddle.

The ref had now left the changing rooms and was carrying the ball towards the centre circle, ready to begin the second half.

Peter addressed the Magpies midfielders quickly: "Look, we have no time for questions or complaints.

"Charlie is hurt and can't run properly. We need to move him into midfield. I'll go up front. Flem can support me and you two can provide the legs. Get the ball to the Boy Wonder and then get moving!"

For once, there were no complaints. The boys merely nodded and ran to take up their new positions.

Charlie limped to his new position in front of the back four.

Annie hissed: "What are you doing?"

Wrecka looked confused too. Charlie answered quickly: "I can't run after that tackle so we're swapping round."

Charlie turned back towards the centre circle before either of them could protest. Peter and Flem kicked off and the ball arrowed straight into Charlie's path.

Ignoring the pain, he swept the ball out to Billy Savage, who was moving forward from right-back.

Billy ran straight into Blooker, who dealt with the danger and looked straight away for Cleatman.

It was at that moment the penny dropped. Charlie realised he would have to mark Colts' world-class playmaker.

Not this time though.

Wrecka read the pass and moved to intercept the ball before it had even got near Cleatman.

The Magpies captain strode out on the counter attack.

Peter pulled several defenders towards the left flank while Flem, who had somehow fallen over, was keeping another Colts player occupied on the opposite wing.

Aware their defence was being pulled in two directions, the Colts central midfielders dropped into the space in the centre of the pitch to protect their goal.

Nobody tracked back with him. It gave Wrecka loads of space.

So he kept going.

And going.

And going.

As Wrecka neared the penalty area, one of the Colts midfielders finally decided to close him down.

The Magpies captain kept his cool and knocked the ball around one side of the Colts player before darting past him on the other.

The unexpected skills by Wrecka caught Colts cold. In desperation, Blooker flung himself towards the ball but it was too late.

Wrecka's trusty right boot thumped the ball hard and low. Charlie saw the net ripple as the home crowd at the far end of the pitch roared in celebration.

GOAL!

Magpies were back in it. 2-1.

Charlie hobbled toward the Mapgies players and caught the end of Wrecka's words.

"… nothing else matters today. Only this. We can do it. We just need to believe."

The smiles on the faces of the Magpies players told

Charlie they were lapping up every word from the skipper.

"One more thing. Charlie is playing deeper this half. Win the ball, get it to him and he'll supply Belly. Keep going Magpies."

They broke away from the celebrations and began heading back towards their own half for the restart.

Adam scowled at Wrecka as the Magpies captain passed him but strangely the Colts striker did not say a word.

Cleatman though stuck out a hand to Wrecka. "Well played, sunshine. That was a beltcr."

Wrecka accepted the handshake and nodded. "Thanks mate."

Charlie had always assumed the entire Colts team behaved like Adam Knight. It seemed he had been mistaken.

The game kicked off again with Magpies throwing themselves into tackles quicker than ever.

Without Emma, they knew they needed to defend deep and catch Colts on the counter attack.

Yet Colts were playing cleverly.

They knew Magpies' energy levels would fall with Emma in the changing room rather than on the pitch.

Barney had returned to the game. He prowled along the touchline and spotted the problem almost immediately.

The Magpies coach called Wrecka over as the ball bounced out harmlessly for a throw-in deep inside the Colts half.

"Great goal, Wrecka. Now we need to change again because Colts are being clever. They're a smart bunch, I'll give them that.

"I assume Charlie is playing holding midfield

because his leg is making it difficult for him to run?"

Wrecka nodded.

Barney kept a hand over his mouth as he spoke so no-one else could hear him.

"A good move. Well done to whoever came up with that.

"Now we have to go all out for the win. This is what we are going to do…."

24. GAMBLE

"Are you kidding me?"

Charlie wrinkled his nose in confusion.

Wrecka shook his head. "No time to explain. It is simple: me, Toby and Billy in defence; you in holding midfield; Greavesy, Theo and Flem in midfield; Peter and Annie in attack."

Peter and Charlie did not say a word.

They were taking a massive risk by taking Annie out of defence. She was one of Magpies' best defenders.

But they were running out of time.

Only ten minutes remained and they were beginning to feel tired. Colts were comfortable – knocking the ball about with barely a care in the world.

Something had to change.

Annie didn't need any encouragement. "Let's do this!" she muttered and raced off towards the other end of the pitch.

From the throw-in, Wrecka smashed the ball

forward long and high.

When Peter had been up front alone, they had to keep the ball on the floor because he wasn't tall enough to win headers.

Now that had changed.

Annie won the header on her first attempt and knocked it to Peter. Only desperate defending stopped Peter from going clean through.

The ball bounced out for a throw but Charlie noticed the difference. The entire Magpies team had moved much higher up the pitch while Colts had dropped deeper.

Charlie had no-one to mark and found himself halfway inside the Colts half.

He watched as Greavesy launched the ball high into the penalty area. This time Annie did not get the opportunity to head the ball.

Determined not to let her win the header, Blooker charged into the Magpies player and sent Annie sprawling.

"PENALTY!"

Charlie screamed with both arms raised. About three quarters of the crowd shouted at the same time.

Everyone looked at the referee.

He did not react.

And then, as if it was in slow motion, he put the whistle to his lips ... and pointed to the spot.

The Magpies players screamed with joy.

Against all the odds, they had been given a lifeline.

Charlie clenched his fists but did not celebrate. He tried to steady his breathing. He knew the responsibility rested upon his shoulders now.

He walked to the edge of the penalty area and scooped up the ball.

The referee was busy booking Blooker for the challenge as Peter helped a wobbly Annie to her feet.

Charlie tried to block out everything. His legs felt like they would collapse at any moment. The blood pounded in his head. He had never known pressure like it.

He placed the ball as the ref began to move everyone out of the box. The Colts goalkeeper said something to him but Charlie blanked him.

He turned and walked back and carefully checked the target inside his mind was working. It was.

As Charlie went to turn towards the goal again, someone caught his eye. Adam Knight had muscled his way to the edge of the area.

They were a couple of metres behind them but Adam spoke loudly enough to be heard.

"You'll bottle it. You're a loser. I know it and you know it."

Charlie looked at the bully. And he smiled.

It was a pathetic wind-up, just like everything Adam Knight did, and it was not going to work.

When Charlie turned back to face the goal, the panic had gone.

He had taken thousands of penalties in his back garden. His mum's fence had been wrecked because of it.

Why was this any different?

Eyes fixed on the ball, Charlie didn't even need to use the magic target that had changed his life so much.

Adam's words ensured he was never going to miss this chance.

He struck the ball with the inside of his right foot, easily past the goalkeeper's despairing dive and right into the bottom corner of the net.

2-2!

Charlie raced to pick the ball out of the net and ignored his teammates' attempts to hug him in celebration.

"Come on Magpies! Keep going!"

Charlie barked out the orders – and no-one disagreed.

They had a game to win and six minutes left to do it.

25. LAST CHANCE

Colts, however, had other ideas. Straight from the kick-off, they were on the attack again.

With Annie up front, there were only three players in the Magpies defence – Wrecka, Billy and Toby – to try to deal with Cleatman and Adam.

Even so late in the game, Cleatman remained a class above.

He took the ball, waltzed past Flem before sliding an inch-perfect pass through to Adam Knight.

The Colts striker shrugged off Wrecka and moved on to the ball in a flash. He was clean through on goal.

Mudder flew out of his area to close him down.

Adam saw the Magpies keeper approaching and chipped the ball early.

Mudder was stranded. He, like everyone else, could only stand and watch.

The shot was perfect. It flew clean over Mudder and began dropping towards the Magpies goal.

Colts fans started celebrating as the ball hit the net.

Adam Knight jumped with joy and began to run to the away fans.

But something was wrong.

The referee did not signal for a goal. He pointed for a goal kick instead.

Then a far louder cheer erupted from the Magpies end as the home crowd drowned out the away fans. Then Charlie realised what had happened.

The ball had missed the goal by a fraction and brushed the side netting to make the net ripple.

Adam and several other Colts players had their hands on their heads at the near miss as Mudder scrambled back to get the ball in play.

Two minutes left.

Mudder's kick went deep into the Colts half and allowed Magpies to move up the pitch.

Annie was beaten to the header by Blooker and the ball bounced into Cleatman's path.

Charlie moved to close the playmaker down. They were in the centre of the pitch.

If he got past the Boy Wonder, Cleatman would have a clear run at the Magpies back line. Charlie couldn't mess this up.

Cleatman brought the ball under control with his chest and turned to face Charlie one-on-one.

He had waltzed past players all afternoon but not this time. Cleatman had tried his step-over trick one too many times.

Charlie read what Cleatman was going to do and nicked the ball from the Colts star before he looked up to begin the next Magpies attack.

It was a pass he never played. Crunch!

Charlie did not know what had happened but he hit the deck with a searing pain in his ankle.

A split second later, Adam Knight joined him on the floor, also rolling around in agony.

The ref blew. "Foul! Magpies free-kick!"

Adam did not try to hide his rage. He could not stand up but started telling the ref off from the floor.

"Nooo! That is absolute rubbish! That moron over there has just tried to break my leg."

He pointed in Peter's direction.

Nigel had seen the whole thing: "You committed the original foul, Mr Knight. The whistle had gone before the second foul was committed. It is a free-kick to Magpies and a yellow card for you."

As the ref held up the card, Adam let out a howl of pain as the physio tried to sponge his ankle. It was clear his game was over.

Charlie was getting to his feet as Peter bounced over. Belly helped Charlie to his feet with a big smile.

Adam could not move but he hissed: "I will get you for this."

Peter ignored him. He turned to Charlie instead: "Now win this for us."

One minute to go. It was now or never.

Everyone was inside the Colts box – even Mudder had left his goal open to charge up the pitch.

If Colts broke away with the ball, there was no-one to stop them.

It was all or nothing for Magpies. Charlie had to get it right.

The crowd quietened down. They knew how important this moment was.

He scanned the angle of the kick. The ball was halfway between the centre circle and the Colts penalty area on Magpies' left wing.

Charlie concentrated on the ball as he waited for

Adam to be carried off the pitch.

Finally he heard the ref's whistle. He placed the target on the inside of the back post and waited for it to go green.

Charlie began the run-up. Four paces.

He connected with the ball perfectly and watched it fizz over the first man.

Wrecka threw himself at the ball but could not connect.

Peter and Annie were both blocked from getting close to the curling cross.

The ball was beginning to dip. It bounced once and kept going towards the far post – exactly where Charlie had placed it.

And then Flem appeared from nowhere.

Unmarked and red-faced, Flem was somehow alone inside the six-yard box. The ball sat up right in front of him. Flem took a huge breath, stuck out his left boot and … missed the ball completely.

Cries of agony could be heard across Manor Park as Flem spurned the golden opportunity to win the game.

But the ball was still moving. It slammed into the post. The Colts keeper was scrambling to get across his goal but the first person to react was the smallest player on the pitch.

Toby ducked his head forward and bundled the ball over the line.

The ref blew his whistle for the goal – and full-time.

Magpies had done it. 3-2!

Their promotion dream was more alive than ever and they would face Hall Park Rovers to decide the winners of the championship.

26. REVEALED

Crowds of people passed the changing rooms. They were singing, shouting and excitedly chatting about the thrilling game they'd watched.

No-one could believe what had happened.

They had beaten a fine Colts team, despite playing the second half with only ten players and no magic football book either.

But it was a magical feeling.

Most of the Colts players had handled the shattering defeat with dignity.

Adam Knight was nowhere to be seen, of course, but Cleatman had congratulated every Magpies player, sub and coach.

When Charlie told him that he was a great player as they shook hands, Cleatman shrugged. "Football's just a game, isn't it? I prefer playing guitar."

And off he had slouched, the best player Charlie had ever seen – and somehow managed to beat.

Once Barney's team talk was over, the Magpies players had raced to get changed and re-join the celebrations with friends and family.

Within 20 minutes, only Peter, Charlie and Annie remained – apart from Barney and Coops who were in the office.

Annie poked her head above the divider that split the girls' section of the dressing room from the rest.

"Have you rung that number yet?"

Charlie shook his head. He had completely forgotten about the mysterious text message with the drama of the match.

"No. I have been kind of busy, haven't I?"

Peter nudged him with his shoulder. "Do it then. Let's see who answers."

Still dripping with water from his shower, Charlie began to rummage in his kit bag to find his phone.

He could feel the butterflies returning. It was only a phone call but it was one of the scariest things he had ever done.

The Boy Wonder found the message and hit the phone icon at the top of the screen.

He waited for the phone to connect.

The wait seemed to last forever.

Charlie could feel the nervous sweat from his hands on the phone.

Finally he could hear ringing at the other end of the line.

Charlie held his breath … and then looked round.

He could hear the ring-tone on his phone as he waited but also from somewhere else in the room.

Peter and Annie looked at each other. Their eyes were wide with shock.

"The phone is in here."

It was coming from the direction of Charlie's bag. Within seconds, Peter had bounded towards the direction of the ringing phone.

A moment later, Peter held aloft the phone in triumph.

He did not smile though.

Charlie cancelled the call and a second later the phone in Peter's hand went silent.

Peter nodded. "Yes, there's now a missed call from your number, Fry. We have finally found the rat."

Annie answered in a whisper. "Who is it?"

The changing room door burst open.

Toby Grace flew into the room and raced straight up to Charlie.

"Charlie, something really bad has happened. You need to know. I …"

Toby never finished the sentence.

Peter grabbed his Magpies teammate around the scruff of the neck so he couldn't move.

Toby looked terrified as a fearsome-looking Peter handed Charlie the phone.

"We know that you're the spy, Toby.

"We've got your phone.

"You've been caught red-handed."

27. DEMON

"What?!"

Toby wailed and tried to wrestle away from Peter's iron grip.

"No, that's not true. That's what I came to say, I found …"

Annie interrupted him. "We found your phone. The one you used to try to discover Charlie's secret. Don't deny it."

Tears began to trickle down Toby's face. He was still wearing his kit after celebrating Magpies's historic win.

"Listen to me please. It's important."

"YOU ARE SUPPOSED TO BE OUR FRIEND! HOW COULD YOU?" Annie's hand shot out and slapped the boy across the face.

Toby looked stunned.

"No, you don't understand."

Peter hissed at him: "Shut it!"

Charlie had said nothing.

He looked at the phone found in Toby's bag,

scrolled down and quickly found the text message conversation.

It had been the phone used to contact him.

He could not believe it.

Not Toby.

Not one of his gang.

Not one of his best mates in Magpies.

And then something stirred in the back of his mind.

"You …" Charlie spoke softly and the others turned to look at him. "You were hiding behind that tree at The Rec when we were talking, weren't you?"

Peter looked deep in thought as he tried to remember the occasion Charlie was talking about.

Annie clicked her fingers.

"That's right. Emma found you when she turned up, didn't she?"

Toby nodded and tried to explain, but Peter spoke before he could get the words out.

"Hang on. Wasn't it you who was lurking outside the changing room doors when we were arguing a couple of weeks ago?"

Toby's eyes widened in horror.

Charlie spoke softly again. "And on the one day I tried to get out of school really early, you were there too."

Peter said: "He's the football spy. What do we do now?"

"NOOOOO!!!! It wasn't me. You have got to believe me!" Toby started to sob. His shoulders were shaking as the tears began to fall on to the changing room floor.

Charlie felt sick.

He had never felt so betrayed.

He did not know quite what to do next.

The changing room door flew open again.

"Wait."

Peter, Annie and Charlie all looked up at the newcomer.

Toby sunk to a heap on the floor, unable to do anything other than sob.

Charlie's nose crinkled in surprise.

It was Joe.

"Let him go. You're making a big mistake."

Peter snorted. "Er, no. We've caught him red-handed."

Joe strode into the room.

"No, Belly, you haven't. You've got the wrong person.

"Adam Knight is the football spy."

"WHAT?!"

Charlie, Peter and Annie looked at Joe like he was crazy.

Joe did not reply. He marched past his three friends and stood as a barrier between them and Toby.

The smaller boy looked up at his saviour.

Joe held out his hand. Toby took it and slowly hauled himself to his feet.

"Cut out the snivelling, Toby. You know you didn't do it. I know you didn't do it.

"Now we have to tell them what has really happened. You can't do that if you're crying, can you?"

Toby nodded eagerly and used the sleeve of his dirty football shirt to wipe his runny nose.

"I …"

Joe sighed. For the first time Charlie realised Joe

looked different. He looked as if he had run a marathon to get here.

Oddly he also had lots of tiny scratches across his face.

"Fine. I'll tell them, Toby, but you had better pipe up when it comes to the details."

Toby nodded eagerly but kept his eyes away from Peter's angry stare.

Belly growled: "Will someone tell us what the hell is going on?"

Joe cleared his throat.

"Okay. Chell Di Santos had been desperately trying to find something, anything, to stop Charlie in his tracks.

"So he struck a deal with Adam Knight: if he found out something bad about you," Joe nodded in Charlie's direction, "then Di Santos would boot Bishop out of Hall Park Rovers and make Adam his number one striker."

Charlie sat down. It was unbelievably harsh. Brian Bishop was a great player.

Annie shook her head in confusion. "Wait, this makes no sense. Why would Adam Knight leave Colts? He is their top goal-scorer by a mile."

Joe cracked a small smile. "Surprise, surprise, they are sick of him already.

"Cleatman told me last week that Knight was history. He will be leaving Colts at the end of the season, no matter what. He had nothing to lose by trying to come after you."

Charlie looked at Joe and moved on to Toby.

"So what's all this got to do with Toby?"

Joe held out his palm to invite Toby to take over the story.

In a small voice, Toby began to speak.

"It was an accident. I was heading towards science one day and he was sitting on one of the benches outside the classroom.

"I heard him talking. I heard Charlie's name clearly. It seemed so odd. Then I heard him say 'Yes, Mr Di Santos."

Toby shivered at the mention of Chell Di Santos. "I knew then it could only be trouble so I decided to follow him.

"Everywhere he went, I followed. He is so arrogant that he didn't even notice. Or at least so I thought."

Toby paused for a moment and looked directly at Charlie.

"He was always following you but at a distance. He was really good at hiding himself – but I wasn't so clever."

Charlie returned his stare.

"So that's why you have been acting so strangely lately? And why we seem to find you lurking around all the time?"

Peter waded in.

"Why did we catch you listening outside the changing room a week ago then?"

Toby nodded, tears still falling from his face.

"Adam was crouching under the window trying to listen to your conversation. I saw him and began running towards the changing room. He saw me and disappeared.

"I was about to follow him but Emma opened the door and everyone thought I was the one listening."

Annie clicked her fingers with a flick of excitement.

"I remember! Didn't he crash into you lot after we had left?"

Toby smiled. "Yes, and by now he knew I was suspicious. I tried to tell you Charlie that same day but he attacked us."

Charlie's mind flashed back to the evening when Adam drove his bike into them.

It was true. Toby had been trying to tell him something. In all the commotion, he had completely forgotten.

"Yes, you were ... I forgot."

Annie held out the phone. "But how do you explain this, Toby? Why were you sending messages to Charlie? I don't understand."

Toby shrugged.

"He stole it. The night he crashed into us, we all went sprawling. He must have pinched it then. I haven't seen it since ... until now."

28. ON THE RUN

The group stood in silence for a moment.

Then Annie stepped towards Toby and handed him back the phone. "He's telling the truth."

Annie hugged Toby.

She whispered: "I'm so sorry for doubting you. Will you forgive me?"

He nodded and returned the hug.

Peter though still looked unconvinced.

"Hang on. What about when Emma found him lurking behind that tree at the Rec?"

For the first time, Toby grinned properly and held his hands up.

"Oh that was nothing. I saw you all deep in conversation and I didn't want to interrupt. I'm not very confident, remember?"

Toby turned his attention back to Charlie. "Do you remember the day you were rushing to leave school early? Somehow he knew you were heading out quickly – and on your own – and was waiting for you outside the gate."

Charlie shivered. He had no idea.

Toby continued: "I had followed him. I saw him disappear and knew I had to warn you. Then those idiots grabbed me.

"Luckily, for both of us, you came to help. By the time we left, there were people everywhere and he couldn't lift a finger."

Charlie remembered only too well what had happened. He knew now.

Toby was telling the truth.

When he spoke again, his voice was strong.

"Toby, I believe you. I am sorry we doubted you. We were wrong. We should have asked you rather than jumping to conclusions."

Toby smiled warmly. "I understand. I would have thought the same thing."

Everyone turned to look at Peter.

Belly stuck out a hand and muttered: "I'm sorry buddy. I…."

Peter's voice trailed off. There were no words.

Toby accepted the handshake.

Silence fell over the room again before Charlie turned to Joe.

"Okay, we've ruled out Toby. But what has Chell Di Santos got to do with all this? And what's happened to you?"

Joe pushed his hand over his scratched face. There were cuts on his arm too.

"I'm fine. I just had to go through a load of brambles to get here as quick as I could. My skin took a battering, unfortunately."

"Where have you been?"

Joe grimaced: "I watched the game with your parents, Charlie, and was hanging around outside waiting for you lot to change. You take ages!

"Then I saw him. Adam Knight scurrying toward the far end of the park towards a lone figure, dressed all in black.

"I knew who it was from 200 metres away. Only Chell Di Santos stands like that."

Joe paused. No-one said a word so he continued.

"I jogged over to the gap in the bushes where the pair of them had disappeared to. They were in deep discussion and didn't notice even when I nearly stumbled right on them.

"From what I heard, Adam Knight only knows a few details but he knows you have a magic target. Chell Di Santos wanted every detail; how it worked; what it did; how you got it.

"Adam didn't know. He only knew you'd got a magic gift that made you great at football. I turned and ran here as soon as they began to move in my direction."

Joe stopped to catch his breath.

He looked at the group of friends in front of him and his voice dropped to a terrible whisper.

"Chell Di Santos knows your secret, Charlie. He is coming to get you."

**

The Football Spy is part four of The Charlie Fry Series. The final book will be available in 2017.

NOTE FROM THE AUTHOR

Time to come clean. The Football Spy is my favourite book of the Charlie Fry series.

Most of us have been there: waiting for the big match; the pre-game nerves; the feeling of sheer joy as you run on to the pitch; the agony and ecstasy of sport. Those moments are precious and – for most of us – are gone before you fully realise how great they are.

I would like to clear up one point: I'm not Charlie Fry. I've never been any good at football and thankfully lightning has never been too close.

But many of the locations are real – Hall Park in Rushden, Northants, remains one of my favourite places – while many of my childhood friends were once outstanding footballers.

The Football Spy concentrates on the importance of being loyal to your friends – and the need to never give up, even if the odds are stacked against you.

Charlie is the Football Boy Wonder but he would never have made it without the help of his friends and family.

They do not treat him differently.

They all treat him exactly the same as the others – with the occasional allowance for his condition. In my opinion, it is the right way to approach friendship.

Like all good things, Charlie's story must come to an end. So the next book – part five of the Charlie Fry series – will be the final part in the main series. I hope you have enjoyed the adventure so far and thank you for all the support. We go again in 2017.

**

Martin Smith lives in Northamptonshire with his wife Natalie and daughter Emily.
He is a qualified journalist and, when he is not writing, he works part-time as a Social Media Manager.
He has cystic fibrosis, diagnosed with the condition as a two-year-old.
The Charlie Fry series is about friendship, self-belief and a love of football – the one sport that seems to unite people of all backgrounds under one cause.

ACKNOWLEDGMENTS

Many hours have been spent creating The Football Spy so I wish to say thank you to those people who helped make it happen.

Mark Newnham designed the book's brilliant cover. Despite his inability to beat me at video games, Mark knows his way around an eye-catching cover.

Football expert and work wife Alicia Babaee helped craft the plot and contributed a heap of changes to help the flow of the story.

Richard Wayte proofread the book to straighten out plenty of grammatical wrong turns.

Sara Wilmot created a wonderful Charlie Fry trailer, which has been viewed thousands of times on Facebook, and inspired me with her endless positivity.

Rob 'The Colonel' Burnell helped keep my fitness up during a tough year. Those miles could not have been much fun but they kept me well enough to be able to write this book.

And lastly my wonderful Gurtie – whose love, patience, tenderness and kindness means more than she'll ever know.

ALSO BY MARTIN SMITH

The Football Spy is part four of the best-selling Charlie Fry Series.

All of Charlie's earlier adventures are listed below:

The Football Boy Wonder

The Demon Football Manager

The Magic Football Book

The entire Charlie Fry Series is available via Amazon in print and on Kindle today.

Follow the series on:

Facebook
Facebook.com/footballboywonder

Instagram
@charliefrybooks

Made in the USA
Coppell, TX
19 February 2021